SPIDER-MOTHER

First Warbler Press Edition 2024

"Sultana's Dream" first published in *Indian Ladies Magazine*, 1905 | "Fifty Miles in an Airplane" first published in *Muezzin* in 1932 | "Fruit of Knowledge" published in its final version in *Motichur*, vol. 2, 1922 | "Burka" first published in *Nabanur* in 1904 | *Woman-Prisoner* first published by Mohammadi Book Agency in 1931 | "True Dawn" first published in *Muezzin* in 1930

"Begum Rokeya" by Akhtaruzzaman Elias translated from *Akhtaruzzaman Elias Racanasamgraha*, ed. Khaliquzzaman Elias, (Mowla Brothers: Dhaka, 2007)
Preface © Mrs. Suraiya Elias

Introduction © 2024 Ben Baer and Smaran Dayal

Translations and Notes © 2024 Ben Baer

Nine illustrations, including cover image, by Chitra Ganesh from *Sultana's Dream,* 2018, Portfolio of 27 Linocuts BFK Rives Tan, 280 gsm, 20 1/8 x 16 1/8 inches (51.1 x 41 cm). Reprinted with permission.
© 2018 Chitra Ganesh, published by Durham Press
Artist's Statement © 2024 Chitra Ganesh

Foreword © 2024 Shahana Hanif

ISBN 978-1-962572-98-9 (paperback)
ISBN 978-1-962572-99-6 (e-book)

Library of Congress Control Number: 2024945596

New York, NY
warblerpress.com

Praise for *Spider-Mother: The Fiction and Politics of Rokeya Sakhawat Hossain*

"In her groundbreaking work of science-fiction, 'Sultana's Dream,' the pioneering Bengali writer, Rokeya Sakhawat Hossain, imagines a world where gender roles are reversed, and women hold leadership positions. With its emphasis on education, technological advancements, and the power of women's leadership, Hossain's work remains vitally relevant today. Kudos to Ben Baer for his fine translations of these important texts."
—Amitav Ghosh, author, most recently, of *Smoke and Ashes: Opium's Hidden Histories*

"A gorgeous, urgent compilation of the feminist, decolonizing vision of Rokeya Hossain, and of her understanding that the best speculative fiction poses a challenge to the violence of the present."
—Siddhartha Deb, author of *The Light at the End of the World*

"Rokeya's uniquely fanciful and didactic mode is brilliantly showcased in this small but significant selection of her writings. *Spider-Mother* offers the added richness of a fresh translation of her Bengali texts by Ben Baer, illustrations to 'Sultana's Dream' by the graphic artist Chitra Ganesh, and an introduction by the editors that addresses, with insight and solicitude, each of the six pieces included in the volume. The result is a volume that will be of compelling interest to readers of feminist, speculative, eco-critical, and postcolonial writing. Those new to Rokeya's writings will discover new worlds in this introduction to a pioneering South Asian woman writer's oeuvre."
—Rajeswari Sunder Rajan, formerly Global Distinguished Professor, New York University

"Efficiently and affectionately introduced and translated, this book will, at last, ferry Begum Rokeya's uncommon imagination to new readers."
—Sumana Roy, author of *How I Became a Tree* and *Provincials*

"This groundbreaking collection introduces readers to the writing of pioneering Bengali educator, activist, and author Rokeya Hossain, much of which is translated to English here for the first time. Featuring Hossain's original speculative stories, journalistic essays, and political manifestoes alongside contemporary illustrations and scholarly essays, editors Ben Baer and Smaran Dayal remind us that the future has always been female, and that feminism and science fiction have always been global endeavors. A must read for students, scholars, artists, and activists alike. Highly recommended!"
—Lisa Yaszek, editor of *The Future is Female!* series and *The Routledge Companion to Gender and Science Fiction*

SPIDER-MOTHER

THE FICTION AND POLITICS OF ROKEYA SAKHAWAT HOSSAIN

Edited and Introduced by BEN BAER and SMARAN DAYAL

New Translations by BEN BAER

Illustrations by CHITRA GANESH

Foreword by SHAHANA HANIF

warbler press

CONTENTS

PREFACE
BEGUM ROKEYA
by Akhtaruzzaman Elias

A story from seventy or eighty years ago. In a village of our country stood the large and grand house of a landlord. One day an outer room somehow caught fire. It was noontime. The mistress of the house was lying down in her room after finishing her meal. On sensing the fire she leaped up. She saw the window of her room was ablaze. She quickly went toward the door to get out. But many people had gathered near the doorway. They had come to put out the fire. Then how could the mistress go there? She is mistress of a great house; can she go out in front of a bunch of men? So she turned and went back into the room. But meanwhile the fire had spread to the room. The clothes rack had caught fire, which spread from the rack to the wooden box. The mistress crouched down and went under the bed. Can one save oneself like this? The bed caught fire in no time. In the blink of an eye the fire had burned the mosquito-net, sheets, mattress, pillow all to ashes and set the bed's legs ablaze. Burning fiercely, the bed collapsed onto the mistress of the house. She could not even scream—she's mistress of a great house—it would be a disgrace for the sound of her voice to reach strangers' ears. Burning in flames, the woman died in silence.

This is no imaginary tale. This heartrending incident is written in a book called *Woman-Prisoner*. In this book you can find many accounts of the suffering and hardship endured by Bengali Muslim women in those days. Rokeya Sakhawat Hossain wrote the book. She did not write books and then just twiddle her thumbs. To the last day of her life she worked relentlessly to eliminate all kinds of oppression, hardship, and wretchedness perpetrated on women.

In those days the women of our country's wealthy Muslim homes were prohibited from leaving the house. Men did not approve of women going here and there independently. All believed that women must remain indoors and only do work around the house. They had no opportunity to read and write.

It was Begum Rokeya who shouldered the burden of eliminating this misery of Muslim women. From childhood she had a powerful desire to learn reading and writing. But at home she faced only restrictions.

She was born in 1880 to a noble landlord family in Rangpur's village of Pairaband. Their house was magnificent, said to be a palace. A many-roomed mansion with valuable furnishings in every room. Numerous guards and staff. It had everything. It lacked only provision for the girls to read and write. The boys studied in school, and when their schooling was finished there was also no restriction on their going to Calcutta to attend college. The objection, then, was confined to the issue of girls learning to read and write.

As she grew up, Rokeya's interest in reading and writing increased. But, in this household, to speak of girls' reading and writing just meant learning a little bit of Arabic. Yet Rokeya's thirst for knowledge was not satisfied by this. But there was harsh punishment if you were caught reading. So Rokeya would read late in the night. Everyone in the house was asleep. Rokeya's elder brother Ibrahim Saber would read in his room with a lantern burning. This one member of the entire household was pleased by Rokeya's interest in studying. Rokeya would get up deep in the night and go to read with him. The brother teaches how to read, and the sister reads with him as if they are one. They read all through the night. Then, right before dawn, she would go quietly back to her own bedroom before anyone noticed.

Once she was a bit older, Rokeya was married to Syed Sakhawat Hossain of Bihar. Her husband was often unwell and Rokeya herself would see to his care. Yet amidst all this, she continued to pursue her own studies. Seeing this disposition for reading and writing on his wife's part, Sakhawat Hossain was, however, filled with joy. He took into his own hands the responsibility for Rokeya learning English.

Rokeya's husband died after only a few years, and she moved to Calcutta. She had faced barriers every step of the way in learning to read and write, and she now resolved to make arrangements for educating Muslim girls herself. Her husband had left her some money, and she used it to found a girls' school. She named it the Sakhawat Memorial Girls' High School.

But once you've started a school, where do you get students? The girls' guardians did not wish to send their daughters to school. They believed that the girls' purdah would be ruined by going outside the home. With many prayers and appeals, Rokeya went from house to house to house pleading with the guardians so that she could fill her school. Some of them heeded her request, and yet others believed it would be a sin because the girls would be seen by all on their way to and from school. Then Rokeya made arrangements for a purdah-covered carriage for them.

Little by little, by the exertion of Rokeya's life's blood, the number of girls in the school began to grow. Moreover, the girls' religious orthodoxy began to wane as they studied in school.

Rokeya's toil for the school was unending. Where could she find time to look to her own bodily wellbeing? Yet amid all this work she also habitually turned to literary writing. She wrote a good number of books. In all these books there are stories of the sufferings of our country's women, discussions of their oppression. And in every book we find the sign of freedom emerging from these conditions.

*   *   *

Note:

This text was written for a primary school textbook by the greatest near-contemporary Bangladeshi novelist Akhtaruzzaman Elias (1943–1997). We include it here to illustrate Rokeya's national significance in Bangladesh as a figure whom the state considers a necessary element in the knowledge of its future generations of citizens. Elias's biographical sketch is among at least five short contributions he made to Bangladeshi school textbooks. The editor of Elias's Collected Works says this about these pieces: "These writings for schoolchildren were printed in the class four textbook, Amar Boi [My Book]...There is no date indicated on the typewritten manuscript. However, it can be surmised that they were written during the latter part of the 1980s."

FOREWORD

by Shahana Hanif

I first read "Sultana's Dream" in 2012 during my undergraduate studies at Brooklyn College. I was a Women's and Gender Studies major,
and it was the first time in the history of my New York City school
career that I was being taught by Black and brown educators, particularly South Asian and Black women and queer scholars. It was in a
required history class that Professor Swapna Banerji introduced my
peers and me to Rokeya Sakhawat Hossain. Growing up, while I heard
about Rabindranath Tagore and Kazi Nazrul Islam, Rokeya Sakhawat
Hossain was not a household name. I was euphoric, reading the words
of a Bengali woman, from well over a hundred years ago.

"Sultana's Dream" came at a pivotal moment in my life: I was
managing the early days of living with lupus, a chronic and degen-
erative autoimmune disease. Diagnosed with lupus at seventeen, the
text ignited in me a desire to interrogate the conditions of first-generation Bangladeshi and Muslim women in the New York City diaspora.
Hossain's vision of a feminist utopia deeply resonated and challenged
my naive notions of feminist exploration as a Western construct.

I grew up in Kensington, Brooklyn, which is now officially recognized as Little Bangladesh. It's an enclave I officially co-named during
my first term in elected office—in one of those seemingly small acts
that end up meaning so much to people who call it home. This neighborhood is home to the largest Bangladeshi community in Brooklyn,
many of whom arrived in the early 1980s, including my father. Ours
is a close-knit, working-class community of families who arrived
through family reunification, the diversity visa program, or through
very risky journeys like my father jumping from a ship. Growing up
in a predominantly working-class, insular Muslim enclave, I found no
trace of Hossain's Ladyland. While Bangladeshi men loitered in the

heart of Little Bangladesh, women and girls seemed to be conspicu-
ously absent. Our ambitions and individuality were often stifled and
forced to manifest in unique ways—a parallel I was quick to recognize
in the worlds that Royeka created for us.

During my 2021 election campaign for City Council, I experienced
Hossain's Ladyland once more. I saw it in the excitement and support of
Bangladeshi women of all ages. My aunties, who had been traditionally
distant growing up, knocked doors in crews of three to four women,
and would greet voters by saying *amader meye daraise*, our daughter
is a candidate, and that it was our *dayitto* to do right by our daughter.
It was hard to take them seriously because this was not historically
my relationship to women my mother's age. However, their activism
and civic engagement demonstrated what they saw in me and it was
clear why they wanted their daughters, like me, to succeed. I was a
vessel for them to leave the darkness of inequity in *The Secluded Ones*[1]
behind. They were breaking free from the gender inequities portrayed
in Hossain's *The Secluded Ones*.

Until my diagnosis with lupus, I was raised with the idea that I'd
be married off early, and while my father entertained the prospect of
me becoming a doctor (his choice, not mine), it was an unsaid truth
in the house that marriage should be my ultimate ambition. I'm not
sure I disagreed. I simply didn't know any Bangladeshi women who
pursued their passions and dreams. Certainly, I knew many who were
married and excellent cooks. But of course Bollywood movies did not
depict women desiring anything more than a romantic relationship
and marriage. And the few aunties who owned and/or worked at store-
front beauty salons and *deshi* boutiques were seen as exceptions. These
aunties were considered *fast,* not my word, but the other aunties who
were privileged enough to be homemakers. Needless to say, although
my mother frequented these third spaces, these women were never
over at our home. As I discovered in *The Secluded Ones,* it was evident
that my choice to settle down would be praised while working in the
pursuit of another kind of life would not.

I felt as though I was living a life of seclusion and frustration,
reflective of Sultana's before her dream. I was *shemla.* I learned that
my caramel complexion (read: dark skin) would be in the way of my

---

1   Translated in this volume as *Woman-Prisoner.*

marriageability. My younger sister's *forsha* skin was worshiped. I was also chubby with a round face, and she was skinny with a defined jawline. I learned to eat less or not at all, straighten or blow out my hair regularly, and accepted that without makeup, I was just not attractive. The characteristics of mine that did get noticed were my black, long hair and how shy and reserved I was. I understood my role in living simply to be accepted by men with all those around me on an assembly line preparing to see me off without my input.

Well, unfortunately for my keepers, my two redeeming qualities of quiet acquiesce and long, black hair were both about to go out the window with my diagnosis. Fortunately for me, however, a stronger, more self-possessed me would be born. It would take immense pain, both physical and mental, but eventually, this version of me would arrive. Of course, I didn't know this at the time. But somewhere along the way, I would discover Rokeya's century-old words, plain as day, telling me I was not alone, and nor was I the first.

I was hospitalized after waiting nearly twelve hours at the emergency room. While no one in my family could predict what would come of this moment, I knew my chances of getting married would now be far more challenging. The pediatric rheumatologist told me that I would not die, but that life would now require "grit." Her words, not mine. The two doses of chemotherapy immediately washed away my beautiful locks, leaving light strands of hair. I hadn't seen my face and body in many weeks, until I was ready to be discharged. When I got home, I never left. I was homeschooled for the final credits required for high school graduation and aside from attending my frequent doctor's appointments, I was in hiding.

I found comfort in writing, much like Rokeya did, to explore the possibilities of breaking from patriarchal norms. I recall sharing an extensive note on Facebook with an update about my diagnosis with lupus. Lying in that hospital bed, I was suddenly struck with the realization that I knew no one around my age living with a chronic illness or disabilities. I couldn't remember my mother or her contemporaries being ill either. Of course they got sick. I just never heard about it. It was as if we were not allowed to be sick.

Once home, motivated by a desire to connect with others and assert my story, I published an online blog called *Shahana With Lupus.* It couldn't be possible that I was the only brown woman confronting physical and psychological pain. I tried to remember characters in novels, television shows, and movies. Nothing. How could that be? It didn't matter to me who would read my entries, it mattered that I didn't die without having told this part of my story. So, I told my story. First to me, then to the world. And once that was done, I started writing the next chapters.

Enter Chitra Ganesh.

Having fully replaced my left hip twice, right hip once, and left shoulder once, I had become a cyborg. When I look at Chitra Ganesh's *Event Horizon,* I see me taking flight as a bionic woman, capable of anything and everything. The convergence of a feminist possibility and resilience. Another brown woman who saw in me what Rokeya saw, what the aunties saw, and eventually, I saw.

Inspired by Hossain's vision of a feminist utopia, my organizing was rooted in making my community safer and inclusive of women. I led efforts to create more open spaces and public plazas in Kensington, such as the Avenue C Plaza, to occupy physical space and exist freely without being burdened by responsibilities. Inspired by the Combahee River Collective, some Bangladeshi sisters and I created the Bangladeshi Feminist Collective—our very own Ladyland. We were a collective of immigrant and first-generation Bangladeshi women, queer and straight, artists, activists, social-service providers, lawyers, and community organizers. No cis and straight men. The Bangladeshi Feminist Collective existed to challenge everything I grew up with.

We arrived as we were, with no looming judgment about how soon I'd be getting married. This was a revolution for me.

ARTIST'S STATEMENT
by Chitra Ganesh

This selection of prints in this book is inspired by Rokeya Begum's feminist science fiction story "Sultana's Dream." Appearing some ten years before Charlotte Perkins Gilman's iconic feminist utopic novel *Herland,* "Sultana's Dream," though not as widely known, holds a singular position among early feminist science fiction literature and in the contemporary mythic imaginary of South Asia. They are part of suite of twenty-seven relief prints that draws from Hossain's vibrant imagery to translate a story written in prose into a visual grammar that speaks to problems that shape twenty-first-century life: apocalyptic environmental disaster, the disturbing persistence of gender-based inequality and violence, the power of the wealthy few against the economic struggles of the majority, and ongoing geopolitical conflicts that cause widespread death and suffering.

My decision to work with linoleum relief prints is informed by the revolutionary role that this medium of printmaking has played in proliferating images and ideas that were once only available to an elite viewership and making them accessible to a broader public. They are historically foundational to the idea of public discourse and social critique, as reflected in powerful and haunting works of artists I drew inspiration from for this project such as Chittaprosad Bhattacharya, Emory Douglas, Kathe Kollowitz, and Elizabeth Catlett. The *Sultana's Dream* print series comments through form and content on this fraught moment in world history, demonstrating the enduring relevance of feminist utopic imaginaries in offering an invaluable means of envisioning a more just world.

The Condition of Womanhood visualizes the moment before Sultana's prosaic musings open up a portal into a remarkable encounter with feminist utopia, in the form of a thriving society in which patriarchal power and its effects are playfully inverted and challenged in vivid detail. I was immediately drawn to how Hossain's story interweaves science fiction, epic myth, and dreams—narrative logics that have long been at the heart of my artistic practice. My works across a wide range of media over twenty-five years center queer and feminist subjectivities in visually dense, temporally layered worlds. "Sultana's Dream" begins as an archetypal mythic journey, with Sister Sara acting as an accompanying guide for the protagonist Sultana's transformative encounters in Ladyland, much as Dante moves through the levels of the inferno with Virgil as his guide in the *Divine Comedy*. Likewise, Hossain's series of spectacularly detailed vignettes, compressed into just a few pages, evokes the density of information one receives in a dream, where vast spatio-temporal tracts are traversed in a matter of minutes or even seconds of clock time.

Images such as *Water Storage* and *Oracle in the Baoli* expand on Hossain's vibrant imagery that imagines future modes of water storage, solar power, and crop cultivation as vital to the conservation of planetary resources. At a moment of unprecedented climate precarity, Hossain's keen focus on societal structures and technologies that steward and extend our natural resources is more prescient than ever. The prints' composition and formal choices reflect a larger methodology of visual research that informs my approach to mythmaking; one which connects and embeds architectures and technologies of the deep past within speculative visions that transport us into the far future. The low mountainous structure featured in *Water Storage* is inspired by the architecture and legacy of Somapura Mahavira, one of the renowned Buddhist universities and centers of knowledge exchange built in the eighth century and located in contemporary Bangladesh. *Oracle in the Baoli* invokes the intricate beauty of the stepwell, a subterranean architectural form and common feature of north and western India from the seventh to the nineteenth century, which functioned as reservoirs and containers for rainwater in exceedingly arid climate. The Baoli as a massive multi-level stepwell embodies a convergence of utilitarian structure and architectural wonder.

We need Hossain's text now more than ever, at a moment when global authoritarianism, political polarization, climate precarity, and economic disparity threaten to foreclose political possibilities.

"Sultana's Dream," and the visual grammar it generates remind us of the radically generative potential of dismantling patriarchy, thinking with structures rather than individuals, the power of collective action, and what a concrete vision of a more just and enduring world might look like.

[*Sultana's Dream*, 2018, Portfolio of 27 Linocuts at https://www.chitra-ganesh.com/work/sultanas-dream]

INTRODUCTION
SPIDER-MOTHER
by Ben Baer and Smaran Dayal

The first—and still the most vivid—biographical account of Rokeya Sakhawat Hossain portrays her at one point as a "spider-mother" (a *makar-mata* or *makarsa janani*). There is nothing sinister in this metaphor. The spider is a figure for the unconditional labor of care and guidance performed by an educator for children that are not her own kin. "Day after day in this way, with the blood of her own breast, spider-mother began to revive hundreds of baby spiders into new life," writes Shamsunnahar Mahmud (1908–1964), a younger co-worker in the girls' school Rokeya founded.[1] Her *Rokeya Jibani* (Biography of Rokeya) appeared in 1937, five years after Rokeya's death. Rokeya's life was shadowed by death: her two daughters died in infancy, her husband died before she was thirty years old, she mourns the beloved elder siblings who took it upon themselves to educate her, and she records examples of the meaningless deaths (literal and social) of countless women in her writings. Yet:

None of Rokeya's own children survived. But she made exteriority into a home. In the twenty-five years of the Sakhawat Memorial

---

[1] Shamsunnahar Mahmud, *Rokeya Jibani* (Calcutta: Bulbul Publishing House, 1937), 63. All translations are by Ben Baer unless otherwise noted. We henceforth follow the conventional South Asian practice of referring to our author by her first name, Rokeya. She is also often honorifically titled Begum (or Begam) Rokeya, as in Akhtaruzzaman Elias's prefatory biography, and she typically published her writings under the name Mrs. R. S. Hossain. Shamsunnahar Mahmud went on to become a teacher of Bengali literature at Lady Brabourne College, secretary of the All Bengal Muslim Women's Society, and an elected Member of the General Assembly in East Pakistan (formerly East Bengal, later Bangladesh) in 1962.

School's life, with the blood of her own breast, she raised the innumerable children of other people into humanity.[2]

Rokeya Sakhawat Hossain (1880–1932) was a major feminist intellectual and activist of the twentieth century and—we are convinced—a voice that translates into the social, political, and cultural environment of the twenty-first. While her writings and institution-building activities are very much of their time and place (colonial India between 1902 and 1932, the span of Rokeya's public interventions in her lifetime), their energy and imagination searchingly reach and call beyond that time and place. They speak to renewed and increasingly universalized urgencies concerning relations between the "religious" and the "secular." They have things to teach us about contemporary debates and conflicts that focus on women's education and emancipation in the non-West and beyond, about persistent misperceptions of Islam as a monolithic bloc, and about the forms that social struggle and critique can take when those who struggle are deeply implicated in and shaped by the very systems within and against which they try to work. This last point is perhaps the most significant: where, she asks, does the (Muslim) feminist woman stand in relation to the script of sexual difference by which she has been written and which she has internalized?

The parenthetic "Muslim" in the last sentence is intentional. It signifies that Rokeya's mindset and ethics were importantly determined by specific practices and tenets of a Muslim household and community, and that Islam remained an indelible spiritual and intellectual resource throughout her life. But it also signifies that she refused to allow her critique to remain limited to a single community or religious idiom. Being Muslim is something she struggled with in both senses of this phrase: first *with* it, using it, as an enabling instrument of reasoned thought and ethical relation. She often invokes Islamic scriptural support for her arguments about women's rights and emancipation, and her work represents an important intervention within this discourse that has many subsequent echoes.[3]

---

2   *Rokeya Jibani*, 105.
3   We would point to the work of Algerian novelist, filmmaker, and activist Assia Djebar (1936 2015) as one among many instances.

And second, in the other sense, *against* it as a system of instituted social practices she believed were perversions of the originary ethos of Islam. Of the perversions, her object is the sex-gender system of (especially upper-class) Muslim society, and in particular the system of sexual segregation/female seclusion and the artificial stupefaction of women by denying them education. As Rokeya knew, and as she repeatedly pointed out with incisiveness and great wit, neither sexual apartheid nor denial of developed intellectual capability to women are problems restricted to Muslim societies alone. To blame them on something called "Islam" is therefore not only factually incorrect, but it also blocks the potential to forge links and solidarity among women of different backgrounds. She thus used the specificity of her own experience and formation to configure a feminist practice (educational and literary) that could speak to much more general and common systems of sex-gender oppression and inequality. The essay "Burka" in the present volume is a good illustration of this, but you can find it everywhere in her writings. The inner knot or complexity of her life and work is in the problem of identifying, naming, disclosing the outlines of a system that is in fact so large and pervasive that as such it is not susceptible to an overall description (i.e., simply to call something "patriarchy"—a word Rokeya does not use—evidently does not solve the problem). That shifting, spectral system inhabits us all, men and women (today we would add queer, trans, and nonbinary) in ways we cannot fully know or recognize. And this poses a problem of speech. It is from within this space that Rokeya speaks and asks to be read and heard.

Rokeya was born in 1880 into an upper-class and conservative Muslim landholding family in rural north-east Bengal.[4] Twenty-three

---

4   The biographical details in this introduction are synthesized from accounts in the following works: *Rokeya Jibani*; *Rokeya Racanabali*; Roushan Jahan, *Inside Seclusion: The Avarodhbasini of Rokeya Sakhawat Hossain* (Dhaka: Women for Women, 1981); Mohammad A. Quayum and Md. Mahmudul Hassan (eds.), *A Feminist Foremother: Critical Essays on Rokeya Sakhawat Hossain* (Hyderabad: Orient Blackswan: 2017); Bharati Ray, *Early Feminists of Colonial India: Sarala Devi Chaudharani and Rokeya Sakhawat Hossain* (New Delhi: Oxford University Press, 2002); Mohammad A. Quayum, *The Essential Rokeya: Selected Works of Rokeya Sakhawat Hossain* (Leiden: Brill, 2013); Kalyani Dutta (trans.), *Freedom Fables: Satires and Political Writings* (New Delhi: Zubaan, 2019); Muhammad Shamsur Alam, *Rokeya Sakhawat Hossain: Jiban o Sahitya* (Dhaka: Bangla Akademi, 1989);

years after the Indian "Mutiny" and the subsequent transferal of Indian sovereignty from a private capitalist corporation to the British state, and five years before the founding of the Indian National Congress that would eventually lead the country to a negotiated independence in 1947. Her formation was in many ways typical for women of the rural Muslim gentry in her time. As Roushan Jahan has observed, strict sexual segregation and female seclusion in Indian Muslim society of the time were markers of class status. It was extremely expensive to maintain a household with separate women's quarters and to supply many varieties of body-covering clothing and shielded transportation.[5] Purdah was a symbol of prestige and a moral imperative internalized and accepted by men and women alike. Moreover, it was to some extent observed within nearly every other religious community in the subcontinent (Hindu, Parsi, Christian). To this practice of seclusion, we must add the uneven nurturing of a certain general social separation of Muslim communities in her generation and the preceding one. This separation or social siloing was partially determined by the aftermath of the so-called Mutiny.[6] This was an experience of defeat for Indian Muslims who had previously constituted the prevailing indigenous ruling class, and the changes included a shift away from Persian as the language of state administration and commerce. The post-1857 years were both a period of retrenchment, occasional rebellion, and reorganization for elite Indian Muslims, but the aftermath also entailed a new sense of community isolation and individuation that had specific effects on gender relations as signifiers of communal difference. Both the British legal system and a variety of—again class-fixed—Hindu, Christian, and Parsi social reform movements were in the nineteenth

---

Motahar Hossain Sufi, *Begam Rokeya: Jiban o Sahitya* (Dhaka: University Press, 1986).

5   Jahan, *Inside Seclusion*, 12. Class is perhaps the one blind spot that we might indicate in Rokeya's thought, though this merits a much more extensive discussion than we can provide here. Her approach to the problems of systemic domination can, indeed, supplement socialist or Marxist perspectives.

6   An uprising that began within the ranks of Indian soldiers of the East India Company (the de facto sovereign power until 1858) who were employed to police the subcontinent. The symbolic aim of the revolt was the restoration of a Muslim emperor in Delhi. The aftermath of this extremely violent conflict subsequently determined the structure of the colony in innumerable ways, including the transferal of the East India Company's sovereignty to the British Crown in 1858.

century looosening restrictions on women's visibility and mobility, but upper-class Muslim society tended toward a more limiting set of norms for Muslim women despite the more liberal Sharia prescriptions for women's rights regarding marriage, divorce, and property.[7] Regarding the matter of class and self-acknowledged status, Rokeya's familial genealogy was ashrafi. That is, an old lineage of elite migrants from Persia whose traditions and language had a complex relation of differentiation from those of the region where they made their homes. Even as they lived among (and often ruled over) a Bengali-speaking population for generations, many ashrafs used Arabic, Persian, and Urdu as languages of choice and deprecated Bengali as a tongue and as a non-Islamic cultural formation.[8] The language spoken in Rokeya's family home was Urdu, and the daughters rote-learned some Arabic through memorization of scripture without knowing the meaning of the words they were repeating.[9] As in many similar situations, women were positioned and ethically obliged to be specific kinds of symbols for the preservation of the integrity and legacy of the community's lineage and self-understanding.

From the start, therefore, Rokeya's experience and position placed her in a complex double bind that she was obliged to navigate on a daily

7   On this point, Roushan Jahan observes that "Islamic *Sharia* laws granted women rights in marriage, divorce, and inheritance of property which were quite progressive for its time. Properly enforced, these laws allowed Muslim women considerable mobility and latitude. Hindu custom in India, following Manu's stricture on the necessity of male guardianship for women in all stages of life, was quite different. This factor may have influenced Indian Muslims in their restrictive attitudes toward women." Jahan, *Inside Seclusion*, 12.

8   This situation was not uncontested within the Muslim community, many members of which advocated more fluid assimilation and the adoption of the majority's Bengali language. The fact that the Muslim upper-class of East Bengal adhered to Urdu as a language of choice in Rokeya's time had remote but definite and agonizing implications when that region was assimilated into Pakistan in 1947. One of the pivotal areas of struggle after Partition was language (and the domination of an Urdu-speaking ruling class over a Bengali-speaking majority), leading to a sanguinary war of independence at the end of the 1960s. In this context, Rokeya's act of becoming a "Bengali" was an astonishingly prescient gesture of peace and coexistence. Shamsunnahar Mahmud is insightful on this point in *Rokeya Jibani*, 112.

9   Rokeya Sakhawat Hossain, "Lukano Ratna" (Hidden Gem), *Rokeya Racanabali* (Collected Works of Rokeya, ed. Abdul Kadir) (Dhaka: Bangla Akademi, 2021), 231–2. Collected works henceforth referenced as *RR*.

basis for her entire life: as an insider on the outside and an outsider on the inside (as a woman and as a Muslim; as a Muslim woman becoming a Bengali Muslim feminist; as an elite Muslim woman subject to restrictions that her social privilege in fact allowed her to transgress and question; such knots can be multiplied). This navigation—in its many twists and permutations—constitutes the "text" or spiderweb of Rokeya's life, and it can be read in each of the writings we present in this volume.

Rokeya acknowledges the singular luck of having one sibling who helped her learn to read and write and another sibling who loved the Bengali language and taught her that love. The first was her elder brother, Ibrahim Saber. In accordance with the gender norms of her environment and the ambitions of her father, Rokeya's brothers were primed to enter the Indian Civil Service by college education in Kolkata. According to Rokeya's first biographer (a co-worker who knew her well and provides invaluable anecdotal information not found elsewhere), Ibrahim gave Rokeya both instruction and encouragement in learning to read and write as well as in more elaborated educational areas. This was by necessity conducted in secret, and Rokeya observes often that she has no formal education whatever.[10] The other sibling was her elder sister Karimunnesa Khanam (1855–1926). In a moving tribute written after her sister died, Rokeya describes how Karimunnesa "learned to write Bengali by scratching marks in the dirt of the yard."[11] As with Rokeya, Karimunnesa's learning-activities were carried out in a somewhat clandestine way with

---

10   *Rokeya Jibani*, 17–19. "I have never entered a girls' school or college," writes Rokeya in the dedication to the first edition of *Motichur* (1904), *RR*, 629. She dedicated that work and her novel *Padmarag* (Ruby, 1924) to Ibrahim, each time acknowledging the teaching he gave her. *Padmarag*, translated and introduced by Barnita Bagchi (New Delhi: Penguin, 2005).

11   "Lukano Ratna" (Hidden Gem), *RR*, 231. This should be connected to the analogous account of the process by which the author of what is considered to be the first Bengali woman's autobiography came to learn to read and write. In her *Amar Jiban* (My Life, 1868), Rassundari Dasi or Devi (1809–99) narrates both her sense of imprisonment in the home of rural east Bengal gentry and her clandestine efforts to learn to read by hiding a purloined page of a book behind her veil and studying it secretly. Moreover, she tells of observing younger boys scratching out their letters in the dirt. The fact that this is the autobiography of a veiled Hindu woman also resonates with Rokeya's argument that the gender seclusion-system is not a "Muslim" issue.

the tacit consent of her brothers. She passed on her knowledge and love of Bengali to Rokeya, a lesson that Rokeya found indelible despite spending much of her life living and working in an Urdu-speaking environment:

> It was through the gift of your loving care that I learned to read the *Barnaparicay* in childhood. Although other relatives had no objection to my learning Urdu and Persian, they were profoundly opposed to my learning Bengali...After living for fourteen years in Bhagalpur without a single person to talk to in the Bengali language I did not forget Bengali, and this is all your blessing. After moving to Calcutta I have been directing this Urdu school for eleven years. Here, too, absolutely everyone—assistants, students, teachers etc.—they are all Urdu-speakers. I have to speak in Urdu from morning till night. But I'm telling you, the fact that despite all this stress I have not forgotten the Bengali language is due entirely to the grace of your blessing.[12]

Karimunnesa was the figure of Rokeya's ideal reader.[13]

Rokeya was married in 1896 or 1898 at the age of sixteen or eighteen (there is not a final consensus on the date). Her brother Ibrahim was instrumental in selecting a husband who could reliably support his sister's intellectual ambitions. The husband, Syed Sakhawat Hossain (1858–1909), was a widowed civil servant whose family home was in Bhagalpur, Bihar. This was Rokeya's base until his death from complications of diabetes in 1909, though she often accompanied him on his working travels, encountering a wide range of people of their class but from different communities and regions. Their two daughters died in infancy, a profound personal tragedy that perhaps played some part in Rokeya's lifelong work of caring for the intellectual and subjective

---

12   "Dedication," *Motichur* vol. 2 (1922), *RR*, 57. *Barnaparicay* (Introducing Letters) is a children's Bengali primer composed by the nineteenth-century civil servant and intellectual Iswarchandra Vidyasagar (1820–91). It is used in many Indian schools to this day.

13   "I no longer enjoy anything now; and I wonder—who will read me?" writes Rokeya at the end of her memorial tribute to her sister. "Hidden Gem," *RR*, 233. It is worth noting that Karimunnesa was a prolific poet, though the notebooks containing her unpublished works have since been lost.

development of others' children. Rokeya began writing seriously, publishing her first essay in 1902 and her first book-length collection in 1904. This first book, *Motichur*, contains signs of the prodigious and penetrating intelligence, macabre humor, and unique prose style that Rokeya would develop in the course of her writing career.

Rokeya had already begun writing about the imperative for girls' and women's education in these earliest essays, and her desire to put theory into practice emerged simultaneously. On his death, Syed Sakhawat Hossain left a monetary legacy partly dedicated to her plans for founding a school for girls. Between 1909 and 1910, Rokeya established a small girls' school in Bhagalpur. Familial intrigues and often-hostile relations with her parents-in-law and with the extended family of Syed Sakhawat Hossain's first marriage caused Rokeya to decamp alone to Kolkata in 1910 where she restarted her educational project as the Sakhawat Memorial Girls' School in 1911. Working against a battery of social and economic obstacles in a situation of high public and mediatic visibility, Rokeya directed, sustained, and expanded the school throughout her life. Her essays, speeches, and letters concerning the practicalities of maintaining her school are worthy of their own volume. A sense of some of the issues involved may be found in sections 13, 17, and 47 of *Woman-Prisoner* in this volume.

Rokeya is best known in the English-speaking world for her 1905 story "Sultana's Dream," a much-anthologized work of speculative science fiction that is one of her few compositions in the English language. It is included in this collection alongside selections from a spectacular 2018 series of interpretive linocuts by contemporary artist Chitra Ganesh. The vast majority of Rokeya's writings are in Bengali. Her first publication was the Bengali article "Pipasha (Muharram)" (Thirst [Muharram]), which appeared in the journal *Nabaprabha* in 1902 and was then anthologized in the above-mentioned book collection *Motichur* (1904).[14] Rokeya left a probably

---

14   Rokeya published a second volume of *Motichur* in 1922. Despite being a colloquial noun, the title presents some difficulties for translation: it is the name of a sweet, a type of laddu or small fried ball. These balls are composed of smaller globules of sugared flour pressed together to make the larger sphere. The word literally means crushed pearls or ground pearls, presumably a metaphor for the small pearl-sized globules from which these confections are made. The title *Motichur* thus connotes both a thing of lustrous beauty for the eye and a tasty treat

uncompleted manuscript on her desk when she died of heart failure in 1932. That brief fragment is titled "Narir Adhikar" (Women's
Rights).

While Rokeya's literary output may seem quantitatively modest
beside that of other renowned writers of her epoch (the *Collected
Works* runs to a little over six hundred pages), it would be correct to
say that writing fiction, prose, and poetry was not her only priority.
And quantity is not everything. She was a profoundly engaged educator and activist for the last twenty-three years of her short life, closely
involved in the establishment and daily functioning of the girls' school
she founded in 1909 and in the activity of a Muslim women's political organization she co-founded in 1916, the Anjuman-i-Khawateen
Islam (Muslim Women's Association). This association linked itself to
the national-level women's movement. The real "text" of Rokeya's life's
work is distributed between these three interwoven yet distinct spheres
of activity. The selections we have included for this volume represent
much of the diversity and range of Rokeya's writings throughout her
career. We have not included writings—including correspondence—
that represent the practicalities of sustaining, publicizing, and defend-
ing the existence of an actual school; of specific educational aims
and pedagogical practices; or of participating in the activity of the
Muslim Women's Association (speeches, lectures, campaigning essays,
polemics).

We have, then, here selected writings that we believe to be exem-
plary of the range of Rokeya's most reflective speculative-fictional and
sociopolitical literature. Each piece uniquely stretches or transgresses
the limits of an established genre or the existing parameters of how a
topic was discussed in its time: the relations between technoscience,
gender relations, and utopian fiction in "Sultana's Dream"; the radical
generality of purdah practices in "Burka"; the potential of Abrahamic
scriptural narrative to allegorize contemporary colonialism in "Fruit
of Knowledge"; the problem of speaking against a system that defines
one's very speech in *Woman-Prisoner*; and the way in which the
manifesto-form can appear under a feminist Indo-Islamic signifier
("True Dawn"). Our selections are arranged in chronological order
except for "Sultana's Dream" (1905)—Rokeya's only work of fiction in

---

for the mouth. An efficient translation might be "pearl-dust" or "pearl-sugar."

English—and its retrospective pendant "Fifty Miles in an Airplane" (1932), which head the collection. As noted above, Rokeya wrote one novel, *Padmarag* (Ruby), that was published in 1924. This important, multi-genre work can be approached as a first experiment in organizing the kinds of materials that Rokeya would present in a different manner in *Woman-Prisoner*. That is, *Padmarag*'s overt plot configures nineteenth-century novelistic clichés of adventure, friendship, and romance such that they work as a framework for the presentation of specific materials representing the experiential, psychological, and social predicaments faced by contemporary Indian women. These range from attempts to navigate domestic and social oppression to the practical details of constructing an alternative institution of solidarity and co-work in which men are marginal figures. *Padmarag* both solicits and subverts the arc of the so-called "marriage plot" and fictively documents the work of an all-female group's maintenance of a multi-faceted institution (school, sanctuary, workshop).[15] At its center is the dramatization of an unconditional ethics of hospitality: a site at which any woman of any background is unconditionally welcomed. Indeed, in principle, unconditionality knows no gender, and the novel begins with the welcoming of a "young man," a "stranger" whose "sister" requires help, and it subsequently depicts the women's unquestioning assistance of two injured men (one of them an Englishman who has murdered two relatives of the female protagonist). In other genres and works not represented in the present collection, Rokeya published articles and entered into correspondence in newspapers and periodicals; she developed a highly unusual and rule-breaking practice of translation into Bengali;[16] she wrote interventions on educational practice;

---

15   It is our strong suspicion that the novel's depictions of letters of complaint, accusation, and threat sent to the directors of Tarini Bhavan (the women-run institution) are, if not verbatim, then closely modeled upon the kinds of resistance Rokeya encountered in running her own school between 1911 and 1932. This "documentary" mode comes to the fore in *Woman-Prisoner* with its conspicuous abandonment of attempts at narrative totalization.

16   As well as a variety of strategic English interpolations translating Bengali words or phrases in her essays, this resulted in three major Bengali writings in *Motichur* vol. 2 (1922): "Light of Islam," "The Murder of Delicia," and "Creation of Woman (Puranic Tale)." For a brief discussion of Rokeya's practice of translation in "The Murder of Delicia," see Ben Conisbee Baer, "What is Special About Postcolonial Translation?" in *Wiley-Blackwell Companion to Translation Studies,*

gave speeches and talks to women's and educational organizations; composed a number of other short stories, social polemics, humorous reflections, and testimonial works; and she published a small number of essays on topics such as rural poverty and precarious indigenous practices of silkworm farming. A small but significant amount of her correspondence has been preserved, and we also know of fifteen poems Rokeya published in various periodicals.

As we noted above, these works deserve their own volume(s). We have included a full translation of Rokeya's most powerful book-length piece of radical reportage, *Abarodh-Bashini* (Woman-Prisoner, 1931), a work that dramatizes the problem of how to construct a feminist critique from within a system and structure whose overall shape and systemic pervasiveness are structurally inaccessible and invisible. The lesson of this work, exquisitely staged through the book's literary organization, can travel to teach political theorists and activists in many other areas. Our hope is that readers will move beyond the present volume and explore further work in other translations and in the Bengali writings.

As exemplified by Akhtaruzzaman Elias's biographical preface to this volume, Rokeya is today a nationally renowned figure in Bangladesh.[17] She is also an increasingly well-known icon of women's rights in India.[18] In Bangladesh, her story is a standard feature of schoolbook

---

ed. Sandra Bermann and Catherine Porter (Hoboken, NJ: Wiley-Blackwell, 2014), 233–45. In the dedication to *Motichur* vol. 2, Rokeya mentions that "The Murder of Delicia" was a great favorite of her sister Karimunnesa. *RR*, 57.

17   The nation-state of Bangladesh, founded in 1971, was part of undivided Bengal during the colonial era. In the partition of 1947 this territory became the eastern wing of Pakistan, provoking mass migrations of Hindu and Muslim Bengalis to either side of the new national border. Linguistic, cultural, economic, and political differences between East Pakistan and the dominant West Pakistani regime produced periods of bitter contestation through the 1950s and 1960s, leading to a war of independence that saw the founding of Bangladesh (literally, "the country of the Bengali language") in 1971.

18   For example, during the 2020 mass protests against the Citizenship (Amendment) Act (CAA) in Chennai, India, a large banner was hung from a building in the Vannarapettai neighborhood during a sit-in that included an iconic portrait of Rokeya alongside the heads of other renowned political figures of India (Gandhi, Nehru, Bhagat Singh, Periyar, Syed Abul A'la al-Maududi, Abul Kalam Azad, Muhammad Iqbal, and Ambedkar). Not only was Rokeya the only woman in this pantheon, but it was one of the first times we have seen her image appear in this way in India. We are very grateful to Harini Kumar for sharing this example

history, and her image is commonly seen in works of popular art across the country. The Bangla Akademi (Dhaka) edition of Rokeya's *Collected Works* has been continuously in print, with updates and enlargements, since 1973.

This book presents a selection of Rokeya's best writing. Biographer Shamsunnahar Mahmud expresses what many readers' initial encounter with Rokeya's literature is like: "My first introduction to her was in the pages of monthly magazines. I remember that even in my girlhood, her straightforward, witty, playful, yet incisive and powerful writing stunned my mind. The self-disclosure in every line of her writing was the annunciation of a new life, like blows beating on the door of an unanticipated vitality."[19]

"SULTANA'S DREAM"

Rokeya's short story, "Sultana's Dream" (1905), is by far her most widely read piece of fiction in the English-speaking world and the one most commonly assigned in college classes. It is also her sole work of fiction in English. While it had come to be taken as common knowledge that the American author Charlotte Perkins Gilman's novel *Herland* (1915) was the first modern work of feminist utopian fiction, that status has been revised through the wider circulation of two other utopian texts: Rokeya's "Sultana's Dream" and the African American author Pauline Hopkins's novel *Of One Blood* (1902–3). And while Hopkins herself was a feminist activist and author, who, as scholar Lena Wånggren writes, "fought to raise consciousness among and further the politics of Black people, especially Black women, in the US and beyond," *Of One Blood* is not a feminist utopia. Moreover, while Mary E. Bradley Lane's novel *Mizora* (1880–81) might count as the first feminist literary utopia, readers are presented with a white supremacist, eugenicist "feminism" in which the "dark-skinned races" have been "eliminated."[20] Therefore, as Wånggren helpfully points out, such a piece of fiction is more appropriately categorized as a *dystopia*, and not a feminist utopia. Which leads

---

with us. A smaller image of Rokeya was also a feature of the protests at Shaheen Bagh in Delhi at this time.

19   *Rokeya Jibani*, 102–3.

20   Lena Wånggren, "Feminist Utopias in the Early Twentieth Century" (2024). *Women's Writing*, 31.2: 314–31.

us back to "Sultana's Dream," the first feminist utopia worthy of the title, a utopia authored by a Muslim Bengali feminist in colonial India.

"Sultana's Dream" begins with the narrator's recounting of a waking dream: "One evening I was lounging in an easy chair in my bed-room and thinking lazily of the condition of Indian womanhood. I am not sure whether I dozed off or not. But, as far as I remember, I was wide awake." In this dream, the narrator, Sultana—arguably, a stand-in for Rokeya herself—is confronted by a woman she takes to be her friend Sister Sara. Sara proceeds to show her around a world unlike the one she is familiar with: most strikingly, there is not a single man to be seen in public space—the men that have survived a terrible war with a neighboring country have voluntarily agreed to be confined in purdah to the zenanas previously reserved for women. In a last ditch effort to win the war, their queen hands over the war effort to the "Lady Principal" of one of the country's universities, who defeats the invading army with the use of a solar weapon. This spectacular defeat serves as a deterrence to future invaders and ends war.

> "Then the Lady Principal with her two thousand students marched to the battle-field, and arriving there directed all the rays of the concentrated sunlight and heat towards the enemy.
>
> "The heat and light were too much for them to bear. They all ran away panic-stricken, not knowing in their bewilderment how to counteract that scorching heat. When they fled away leaving their guns and other ammunitions of war, they were burnt down by means of the same sun-heat. Since then no one has tried to invade our country any more."

Once the men are habituated to the separated realm of the zenana, they eventually come to accept it and are consigned to domestic tasks such as cooking and childcare. The narrative invents a terminological reformulation to signify the reversal of the social roles of men and women in its fictional scenario:

> "Now that they [the men] are accustomed to the purdah system and have ceased to grumble at their seclusion, we call the system 'Murdana' instead of 'zenana.'"

That is, the name of the appropriately enclosed place is switched from one signifying what befits woman ("zan") to one with a polysemic range in Indic Perso-Arabic, a place for men or even corpses. Rokeya's English typography allows this play with her neologism for the men's quarters.

Having ceased to complain, the men come to accept their new secluded place in society. Moreover, through Rokeya's thought-experiment, we are able to see the system of purdah abstracted and generalized from its specifically gendered character as a social system of seclusion hitherto arbitrarily imposed on women. Such a framing is, in fact, not unlike Rokeya's own interpretation of the meaning of purdah in her essay "Burka," included in this volume. "Burka" de-exceptionalizes and de-orientalizes the practice of purdah as an aspect of a generalized privacy or discretion: it is not that purdah is a sign of an oriental despotism that needs to be abolished along with everything associated with Indo-Islamic culture. It should rather be understood as oppressive and harmful in its current, misogynistic form.

What we are left with, then, is a world turned upside down. In an anticipatory echo of Frantz Fanon's conception of decolonization as a "program" to "turn...society...upside down," in "Sultana's Dream," we are presented with a depatriarchalized society, one quite literally turned upside down—or inside out—by the substitution, not of the colonizer with the colonized—the British are entirely absent from the narrative—but of men with women. And unlike the society of the Amazons of Greek myth—Herodotus's Androktones—or the world of Gilman's *Herland*, the men in Sultana's society have not been vanquished, slain, exiled, or bred out of existence through parthenogenesis, but rather, as Sister Sara tells Sultana, consigned to "their proper places, where they ought to be."

The remainder of "Sultana's Dream" illustrates the spectacular results of this role reversal: epidemic diseases have been eradicated; premature death (except by accident) is no longer a fact of life; food is no longer cooked with the use of wood or coal but with clean solar stoves; the streets are not paved, but formed of flowers and moss; "early marriage" has been abolished; women are educated as a rule and there are all-women universities; the country has managed to develop zeppelins, harvest water from the sky through a kind of cloud-seeding, invent flying cars, and generate electricity from solar energy. Let's pause to catch our breath. Remember, Rokeya was writing this in 1905. The Zeppelin had just been invented and the Wright brothers had only just taken their first flight. Aleksandr Stoletov's development of the first solar cell had happened at most a decade and a half earlier. It was an exciting time to be alive—but the impact of most of this technology had yet to affect the lives of most people in the world. "Sultana's Dream" was engaged in a visionary kind of science fiction, one that not only prefigured the effects of these brand-new inventions and discoveries on society, but also undertook a kind of sociological speculation that reimagined the very relations between people (gendered, colonial, economic, etc.) that constituted society itself.

Rokeya was not content with simply reimagining the workings of gender in society. She ends her story with the extension of the patriarchal logic of early twentieth-century colonial Bengal to that of European colonialism:

> "I was very much delighted to make her [the Queen's] acquaintance. In the course of the conversation I had with her, the Queen told me that she had no objection to permitting her subjects to trade with other countries. 'But,' she continued, 'no trade was possible with countries where the women were kept in the zenanas and so unable to come and trade with us. Men, we find, are rather of lower morals and so we do not like dealing with them. We do not covet other people's land, we do not fight for a piece of diamond though it may be a thousand-fold brighter than the Koh-i-Noor, nor do we grudge a ruler his Peacock Throne. We dive deep into the ocean of knowledge and try to find out the precious gems, which nature has kept in store for us. We enjoy nature's gifts as much as we can."

In this utopian society of Sultana's dream, not only does the reconstituted (and decolonized) feminist society refuse to trade with countries who continue to confine, seclude, and oppress their women, but it refutes the very logic underpinning those other societies, one that "covet[s] other people's land," "fight[s] for a piece of diamond...a thousand-fold brighter than the Koh-i-Noor," and one that "[be]grudge[s] a ruler his Peacock Throne." The references here are, of course, to the

Koh-i-Noor diamond, one of the world's largest, appropriated by the British and given to Queen Victoria in the wake of the Second Anglo-Sikh War (1848–49), and the Peacock Throne of the Mughal Empire, which went missing during the looting of Delhi's Red Fort following the Indian Rebellion (or Sepoy Mutiny) of 1857. Rokeya is very clearly locating the feminist utopia of "Sultana's Dream" in opposition to the British Empire and its colonizing, expansionist, and acquisitionist logic, while simultaneously framing that logic as an inherently patriarchal and masculinist one: the countries who sequester their women are precisely those that colonize. In her second work of speculative fiction we include in this volume, "Fruit of Knowledge (A Fable)," we similarly see her exploring these interconnected themes of colonialism and patriarchy.

It should be said that "Sultana's Dream" did not receive universal praise, nor did it go uncontested, even within the nascent women's movement in South Asia. In a later issue of *Indian Ladies Magazine,*[21] a woman writing under the pseudonym "Padmini"[22] offers readers an alternative ending to Rokeya's story. In a remarkable kind of revisionist fan fiction, Padmini's "An Answer to Sultana's Dream" envisions a scenario in which various women in the utopia of "Sultana's Dream" now find themselves bereft and wanting after the relegation of their men to domesticity. Some, we are told, are "tired" because of "the office work and the political worries." They no longer dress well, they tell their queen, as "[t]here are no men to admire us." Others are "sad" and have "tear-stained faces," because the men of Ladyland—now referred to as "servants"—are no longer capable of "comfort[ing]" them. Two final groups of women are described as "angry" and "frightened." The former because their children no longer come to them, preferring the men who spend more time with them, and the latter as a result of "a rumour that a new enemy is coming" to invade Ladyland.

Rokeya's feminist utopia, in Padmini's rewriting, has failed. Society

---

21   Padmini, "An Answer to Sultana's Dream" (1905). *Indian Ladies Magazine,* V.4: 115–17.

22   The scholar Deborah Anna Logan notes that "Padmini" is a pseudonym and "unrelated to Padmini Satthianadhan (b. 1905), whose writing was featured after 1927, when she became ILM's assistant editor." (*The Indian Ladies Magazine, 1901–1938: From Raj to Swaraj,* Bethlehem, PA: Lehigh University Press, page 57, footnote 10)

is only redeemed when the men lie to the women, telling them that "[t]he babies are sick," causing the majority of the women of Ladyland to defect to domesticity. The men then return to the public realm to fight off the new enemy—the rumors of war, we learn, were true—and "annihilate" this technologically superior "foe." In effect, war and lies combine to restore male domination. What's fascinating about Padmini's fan fiction, however, is that she insists that men and women now enjoy "equal rights" and are "on an equal footing," even as women have once again been returned to domesticity. "Let the women do what they are fitted for and the men what they are fitted for," a group of "sweet-looking women" tell the queen in the wake of this second war. "And let us have equal rights in everything." Not only does Padmini take Rokeya's thought-experiment in "Sultana's Dream" literally, arguably missing the subtle critique Rokeya is staging of purdah in the speculative register, she also attempts to remedy this fictional oppression of the men of Ladyland by simply re-reversing the roles. We are never told what this newfound equality of the genders means in practice: everything is as it always was and will be.

Finally, in "Sultana's Dream," we see the elevation of women professors and university directors—"Lady Principals"—to leadership positions within Ladyland and the mass mobilization of students in the military defense of the country. They advance from the governance of higher education to that of the country. It is the female University Principal and her female students whose inventions and interventions stop warfare conducted by men, make further warfare impossible, and transition to governance of the henceforth peaceable country.

There is at least one uncanny contemporary resonance from these fictional images today: the Bangladesh protests of 2022–24, culminated in the resignation of the country's prime minister, Sheikh Hasina, and the appointment of students to ministerial and other roles in the country's interim government.[23] Moreover, there is a terrible irony in the fact that the violence perpetrated by police against student protestors on the grounds of Begum Rokeya University, in Rokeya's home state of Rangpur, led to the death of a twenty-three-year-old student,

---

23 Now led by Nobel Laureate Muhammad Yunus, while students such as Nahid Islam and Asif Mahmud have been catapulted from the university classroom into leadership positions in the Bangladeshi government.

Abu Sayeed. For Rokeya, it was women educators and students who held the greatest potential in shaping her utopia, and who were its most capable leaders. In contrast, Ladyland is an abolitionist's dream: it has done away with its police and military.

"FIFTY MILES IN AN AIRPLANE (DREAM FULFILLED)"

"Fifty Miles in an Airplane" offers a retrospective look at "Sultana's Dream" and a glimpse of the distance Rokeya had traveled into a modernizing world since she wrote that story. It was published in the Bengali-language periodical *Muezzin* in 1932, very near the time of Rokeya's death and a little over a quarter-century after "Sultana's Dream." The subtitle, "Dream Fulfilled," indicates Rokeya's humorous and moving assertion that the "dream" she had dramatized in her 1905 story—a dream that included powered flight—had become reality. The essay recounts the first two responses Rokeya received for "Sultana's Dream" and then tells the story of her first and only experience of air travel in late 1930. With a light touch, this brief piece makes several interesting points. It allows Rokeya to affirm that her science fiction story had a genuinely prefigurative element: "At the time I wrote 'Sultana's Dream,' there were no airplanes or zeppelins in existence; motorcars had not even reached India yet. Electric lights and fans existed in an imaginary future. I, at least, had never seen any of this at that time." In other words, "Sultana's Dream"—as speculative fiction written in isolation in semi-rural Bihar—was sufficiently resonant with actual currents of historical development such that it could give a prefiguration of technologies that did actually emerge in the future. While technological development is driven rapidly by capital and warfare (hence airplanes), transformation of society's gender relations is a far slower and more intricate process. But even here she sees certain signs of progress: "I had really traveled in the air as I had described twenty-five years earlier in 'Sultana's Dream.' It was me: I was the first woman-prisoner to have flown with Bengal's first Muslim pilot." The essay subtly marks the different rhythms and temporalities of social change and technoscientific development, ending on a note that acknowledges the ongoing daily struggles of women. But it also shrewdly implies this: if the technoscience part can "come true" in only a quarter-century, then the realization of the "dream" of a future epoch of gender justice must be imagined, and worked for, as equally possible.

"FRUIT OF KNOWLEDGE (A FABLE)"

"Fruit of Knowledge" (*Gyanphal*) counts among a number of significant works of speculative fiction written by Rokeya in Bengali. It and another story, "Fruit of Freedom" (*Muktiphal*), were initially published in 1907, but expanded later in 1921 for inclusion in the second volume of *Motichur*. Both stories can be thought of as allegorical fables and were described by her in Bengali as *rupakatha*, a term used to denote a fairy tale or a fantastic story. "Fruit of Freedom" is an allegory of the formation and tensions within the Indian National Congress, the political party that would go on to win India's independence from the British half a century later. "Fruit of Knowledge," meanwhile, similarly uses Abrahamic scripture and allegory to critique British colonialism in South Asia and the role of indigenous patriarchy in weakening resistance to foreign rule. Both draw on the Islamic cultural mythology of jinns as part of their narratives.

The story reinterprets the scriptural narrative of Adam and Eve. It uses that frame narrative to explore issues of gender oppression, access to knowledge, exploitative trade relations, and colonialism. However, Rokeya adds a cautionary note to preempt objections from conservative religionists: "I have not here followed the events as described in the Holy Quran or the Bible."

The first part of the story remains closest to scripture: Adam and Eve dwell in the Garden of Eden, they enjoy a life of abundance, and God prohibits them from eating the fruit of a particular tree. However, there is no snake that tempts Eve into eating the forbidden fruit—she simply happens to, without agonizing over its implications. Having eaten the fruit, she gains a knowledge that makes her self-conscious about her nakedness and is burdened with a sorrow she had not known before. Having been convinced by Eve to also eat the fruit of knowledge, Adam begins to see his predicament in the Garden of Eden as that of a "captive" trapped by God "in a gorgeous palace," not unlike, we might add, the more affluent women confined within the system of purdah. The pair are then "consumed by an unknown possibility for some kind of transformation." After confronting God and being banished from the Garden, the two live "the real life of a couple."

At this point, there is a further divergence from scripture and the emergent signs of a feminist sensibility. Whereas Eve is able to endow her daughters with a range of strengths and capacities, Adam's sons inherit no extraordinary characteristics from him—he lacks the "will-power" to endow them with advantages:

> Eve loves her daughters intensely, makes her female line live long, sets them up in happy, peaceful homes; amasses an inde-structible store of love in their hearts.
>
> Adam, too, cared for his sons deeply, but his willpower had no such strength and he did not give his sons any special gifts.
>
> With mother Eve's blessings, her clutch of daughters, once born, grew twice as strong, lived four times longer! And Adam's favorite sons, once born, raised too indulgently, were twice as susceptible to sickness and four times more likely to die! When they did not die naturally, they killed each other fighting in wars and battles! They rotted away in prisons and suffered many agonies!

Much as in "Sultana's Dream," Rokeya posits a male propensity for war and aggression, exacerbated by their being "raised too indulgently," and leading them to be more likely to fall sick, die in battle, or end up imprisoned.

Having given us this quasi-scriptural frame, Rokeya is able to delve into the story she really wants to tell, that of a colonial encounter between two peoples. We learn that when Eve is banished from Eden, she "tosse[s] her half eaten fruit of knowledge down to earth" from whose seed "a great tree [is] born in the east of the world." The entirety of the story from this point on revolves around the powers that this tree is able to endow on the various peoples of this world. On the one hand, we are told that a country of spirits called Faerieland (*Paristhan*) exists on one side of a great ocean. Its inhabitants are exceedingly wealthy, but "they burn with starvation," since the only food that grows on their land is the attractive yet virtually inedible makal fruit. On the other, we learn that there exists a land of abundance with "flourishing cities" called Golden Island (*Kanakadwipa*), filled with "many species of trees with delicious fruit, among which groves of mangoes predominate." The jinn (male inhabitants of Faerieland) discover Golden Island on a journey to find other nations with which to trade.

By convincing the "highly civilized, saintly natured people" of Golden Island to trade with them, the jinn begin a years-long unequal and exploitative exchange with the people of Golden Island, leading to a famine in that country. Finally, by accidentally consuming guavas from Faerieland grown with "water mixed with juices of the fruit of knowledge," the Golden Islanders break out of the psychological spell they have been under. This leads to a burgeoning consciousness of their condition among the islanders:

> They looked around in wide-eyed amazement and saw that the jinn-folk had taken everything from the land in exchange for a single kind of fruit; now, like leeches, the jinn-folk were sucking out whatever blood was left! Their hearts were torn apart at the wretchedness of Golden Island.

Having achieved a level of clarity about their predicament, the islanders decide to cease their trade with the jinns, which throws "Faerieland's commercial associations into chaos." Seeing that the islanders are now able to feed themselves with the guava tree they have cultivated, the jinn attempt to destroy that tree. The islanders then send out a mission to locate the original tree of knowledge that grew on this world from Eve's half-eaten fruit and to bring back its seeds to Golden Island.

The story concludes with the islanders discovering that the original tree of knowledge has perished, because,

> the blinkered, selfish scholar-fools of this land prohibited women from partaking in the fruit of knowledge. In due course this prohibition was taken as a social law and the men monopolized this fruit for themselves. The great masses of women forbidden to gather and eat the fruit turned away from nurturing the tree. Without the tender care of women's hands, the tree gradually died!

The islanders return to their homeland and to build a society that places women at its center as cultivators and equal members, leading to the jinns' inability to stop Golden Island from returning to prosperity and, thus, their irrelevance.

> Thenceforth Golden Island was once more doubly and trebly replete with prosperity; its inhabitants passed the time in utmost happiness. They will not be misled by any more deception! Because now women are guardians of the garden of knowledge.

The story may be read as an allegory of India's colonial situation built on an exploitative trade relation. Not so much the British Raj at its height in the late nineteenth and early twentieth centuries, ruling directly over India, but its predecessor, the East India Company before the Indian Rebellion of 1857, which impoverished the subcontinent through extractive trade relations and hostile governance. Most strikingly, however, the famine on Golden Island would immediately bring to mind, for any contemporary reader of Rokeya's, the Bengal famine of 1770, as a result of which seven to ten million Indians are estimated to have died, as a direct result of crop failure and the East India Company's actions.

What may be more significant about "Fruit of Knowledge," however, is not so much its ability to render the colonial situation in a speculative and/or fabulative register, but rather its understanding of the interdependence of gendered and colonial oppression along with its vision of resistance to both. The Golden Islanders' successful delinking from Faerieland depends, in Rokeya's account, entirely on a transformation of its gender relations. It is hard not to hear in the concluding sentence of the story—"now women are guardians of the garden of knowledge"—both an emphasis on the importance of education to the women's movement and an anticipatory echo of an ecofeminist politics of the kind later seen in the *chipko* movement of the 1970s and that championed by the Indian scholar-activist Vandana Shiva, who urges us to see rural and indigenous women as the stewards of ecological sustainability and diversity. In a short essay titled "The Peasant's Sorrow" (*Chashar Dukkhu*, 1920),[24] Rokeya similarly asks us

---

24 The essay was recently translated and anthologized by Kalyani Dutta in the

to train a critical eye on the ambivalent consequences of modernization and calls for the revival of "native industries—especially women's industries." The Golden Islanders, in this story, are not simply fighting the economic rule of the jinn, they're also resisting the monocropping of their lands and the destruction of their ecological and agricultural diversity.

Relatedly, the islanders' boycott of Faerieland imports in no small part indexes the then-nascent Swadeshi movement, which began in 1905, just a couple of years before the publication of "Fruit of Knowledge," at Calcutta Town Hall. Although the movement is more often remembered through its later association with Mahatma Gandhi's public burning of imported English cloth in Bombay in 1921, it had arguably become part of the subcontinent's collective consciousness decades earlier.

In short, Rokeya's speculative fiction, whether in "Sultana's Dream" or "Fruit of Knowledge," uses the fabulative register to anticipate aspects of a postcolonial ecofeminist politics. Far before other writers would receive greater recognition and acclaim for putting speculative and science fiction to work in addressing the structural harms of gendered, racial, and colonial oppression, and imagining liberated futures, Rokeya was writing both technological and emancipatory futures that were very far—but powerfully extrapolated—from the lived reality of women in turn-of-the-century colonial Bengal.

"BURKA"

The essay "Burka" was first published in the monthly journal *Nabanur* in 1904 and was included in Rokeya's book collection *Motichur* vol. 1 that year. It is an important text for several reasons. In this essay, Rokeya begins to develop an important distinction that constitutes an essential philosophical, ethical, and political thread of her subsequent work. This is the distinction between purdah and systemic imprisonment/seclusion (*abarodh*). Rokeya argues that some kind of self-seclusion or veiling is an "ethical" rule, presupposed by and definitive of human civilization, distinguishing the human from animal life. This is a kind

volume *Freedom Fables: Satires and Political Writings* (2019), New Delhi, India: Zubaan Press.

of universal, a point that Rokeya makes by saying that "purdah"—as an instance of seclusion—means non-disclosure, covering, or privacy. She adds that this generalized purdah takes different forms in different cultural systems, as practices and habits of a certain idiomatic etiquette or discretion: "In the present era, our European sisters have ascended to the very limits of civilization; who can say they do not have purdah? No one can enter their bedchambers or even their sitting rooms without permission." She humorously and profoundly illustrates this universality: letters in envelopes (private contents), curtains, lids to cover food servings, tablecloths, pillowcases, as well as the private chambers of a house (a room of one's own). The burka, then, is but one example of the variegated types of "privacy" or non-disclosure that define the development of human civilization. It is in principle no more inconvenient or cumbersome than "the gigantic hats worn by Englishwomen" (one could today translate this into the time and effort spent on beauty regimens. If we "put our face on" to go out, is this not a covering that presents itself to the world?). And it is also an acknowledgement of sexual difference and desire as they structure and play across social space: "it is our belief that no respectable woman wishes to attract hordes of gawkers as she waits on a railway platform." The morality and terminology here may seem old fashioned, but think about it. In which contexts might you wish to not be constantly surveilled?

Given that a generalized purdah characterizes civilization as such, Rokeya finds it absurd that an item of clothing that can cover head, face, and body (the burka as a portable instrument of the very privacy valorized by civilization) should be singled out as in itself detrimental to women's progress and emancipation. While we cannot elaborate on the point here, this argument speaks in prescient and relevant ways to recent conflicts about "the headscarf," especially in contemporary France and Britain.[25]

"Yet every rule does have its limits," writes Rokeya. It is here that the distinction between purdah and a kind of imprisonment appears— where imprisonment is the instituted excess of the universal decorum

---

25   For excellent recent discussion of these questions in European contexts see Joan Wallach Scott, *The Politics of the Veil* (Princeton: Princeton University Press, 2007) and Emma Tarlo, *Visibly Muslim: Fashion, Politics, Faith* (London: Bloomsbury Academic, 2010).

that is called "purdah" by Muslims and "privacy" by Westerners. Women have become the subjects of an "unjust purdah" that translates purdah's harmless politesse of privacy into a rigid system of sexual apartheid (indeed a system that segregates women from other women as well as from men). What matters is the development of a practice and habits that negotiate the shifting and strategic points at which privacy gets hardened into a system of apartheid. Rokeya believes that in her environment women's education is the most crucial point of intervention because sexual apartheid entails the systemic and artificial intellectual underdevelopment of women, and their consequent inability even to comprehend the outlines and laws of their oppression. The wearing of a burka does not hamper intellectual development. Indeed, she concludes, zealous reformers who fetishize it as a symbol of Muslim backwardness that must immediately be abolished will in fact deprive young women of the very educational access that such reformers claim to propagate.

WOMAN-PRISONER

Woman-Prisoner is in one sense a report—or series of reports—from the frontline. But the concept of a frontline implies a clearly identifiable conflict, the boundaries of which are legible and the opposing parties recognizable. This unique and unclassifiable work both inhabits the genre of reportage and questioningly expands it into something else; something more uncanny, mysterious, and challenging. How to report on a conflict that is millennially ancient, that defines the social order, that we are born into without either choice or knowledge of which "side" we are on? How to speak to something that not only does not have an identifiable face or persona, but whose laws already subject the speaker? Consequently, Rokeya writes at the beginning of *Woman-Prisoner*, "For a long time now we have become accustomed to living in prison. Thus we—and especially I myself—have nothing to say against prison. If you ask a fishwife, 'Is the stench of rotten fish good or bad?' what will she reply?" The stench of rotten fish is unrecognizable to the fishwife: she inhabits something that does not register in her perception or consciousness. Perhaps she would reply to Rokeya's imagined question, "What the hell are you talking about? What stench? Are you trying to insult me?" And this is Rokeya's point. There is no shared and secure point of reference for these interlocutors. Rokeya speaks in this text *as* the fishwife or the prisoner who knows no other environment. Not having a place of mastery and overview from without, she too is inside the stench-that-is-not-a-stench or the cell that feels like home. As are we all, in one way and another. And to speak from within ("we have become accustomed to living in prison…I…have nothing to say against prison") means finding another way to speak.

Elsewhere, Rokeya makes this point as follows:

> I have no desire to express my own opinions on purdah—I will just say this one small thing, that I do not agree with Mr. Sheikh [Abdullah] that it is "the most agonizing of all wounds." If it were "agonizing," women would split the heavens with screams of pain, "Oh no! Help! I'm dying! It's killing me!" The seclusion-system can be compared with deadly carbon monoxide gas. Because carbon monoxide gas kills painlessly, people have no opportunity to take preventative measures. Little by little, women living in the inner quarters are dying from this seclusion gas, silently and without suffering.[26]

This is why Rokeya speaks "as" the prisoner or fishwife but not from the standpoint of claiming that "I know this prison and because of that I can speak better than anyone about it." Rather, "I make a gift of describing some of our personal experiences." The situation demands an oblique, anecdotal form of address that multiplies, and offers as a gift, singular examples of an uncanny, pervasive thing that has invisible outlines.

Woman-Prisoner was first partially serialized as a series of "sketches" in the monthly journal *Mohammadi* between 1928 and 1930. The complete version presented here in translation appeared as a book in 1931 published by Mohammadi Book Agency of Calcutta. The Bengali title of the book is *Abarodh-Bashini*. "*Abarodh*" stems from the Sanskrit *rudh*, a verbal root with many meanings that include to block, obstruct, hem in, confine, lock up, besiege, occupy. Its field of meanings is thus invested with (indeed occupied by) implicit relations of power, force, or

---

26   "Bengal Women's Education Association (Presidential Address)," *RR*, 229. The speech was delivered and subsequently published in 1927.

violence: the capability of restrictively controlling the environment or movement of another entity (persons, cities, territory, animals, rivers, etc.). As a Bengali noun, *abarodh* has a similarly broad range within this field of force: confinement, seclusion, imprisonment, blockade, siege. *Abarodh-pratha* (seclusion-system) was a colloquial term in that language for the diffusely instituted practice of female segregation and isolation. Rokeya uses it frequently in her writings, and depending on context and usage she makes its connotations stronger or weaker. Here she gives it the strongest possible formulation, which is why we have chosen prison/imprisonment for the translation. Throughout the text, Rokeya qualifies her object in terms of jail cells, incarceration, and being an inmate. *Bashini* is the feminine-inflected term for an inhabitant, a woman who lives in x or y place. *Abarodh-Bashini* thus means a female inhabitant of a prison, place of confinement, or place of seclusion. Honoring the argument of this particular text, we take the liberty of translating it as "Woman-Prisoner."

It is in this work that Rokeya confronts, in her most philosophically and politically developed way, the problem of finding a critical place from which to write and speak. That said, this is not a conventional work of theory or political analysis. Rokeya's text demonstrates that "speaking truth to power" is the comfortable and illusory privilege of those who think themselves to be outside the power-system they criticize. If this "power" is everywhere, working in and through us in ways we do not know and cannot perceive, it splits us from within and denies us the privilege of distance. This situation demands a mode of speech that is in turn (or at once) anecdotal, confessional, experiential, mocking, depressive, "tragicomic," ranting, sarcastic, and so on.[27] Indeed, this kind of speech can have no stability of genre but is condemned to endless repetitions of the "same" thing in many voices and modalities.

Despite this intrinsic instability, Rokeya finds a striking framework within which to structure her forty-seven numbered episodes or incidents. Almost every one begins with what seems to be a straightforward

---

27   Our argument here is informed by Dina al-Kassim's notion of the "literary rant" in al-Kassim, *On Pain of Speech: Fantasies of the First Order and the Literary Rant* (Berkeley: University of California Press, 2010). See also the brief and related comment on Rokeya in Gayatri Chakravorty Spivak, *An Aesthetic Education in the Era of Globalization* (Cambridge: Harvard University Press, 2012), 151–2.

statement of fact: "A house caught fire" (#8); "A wealthy man of the Bihari gentry was traveling to Darjeeling" (#16); "One evening a gentleman was pacing the busy platform of Sealdah Station as he waited for a train" (#22); "In principle, even our names observe purdah" (#26); "About eighteen years ago in Calcutta, a one-and-a-half-year-old infant had come down with fever" (#33). In each case, this terse initial statement unravels into a bizarre, inexplicable, excessive, uncanny, or grotesque episode; an episode that, through the very power of repetition, should make us ask why the "same" things keep happening again and again. From daily small humiliations, misunderstandings, and embarrassments (today one might add "microaggressions") to instances of isolation, hostility, terror, psychological manipulation, physical violence, and death.

In the rhetorical force of litany or (excessive) repetition, *Woman-Prisoner* registers the logic of a pervasive system and the desire to disclose it in a coherent narrative. But such all-pervasive systematicity does not lend itself to coherent narrative formalization; rather, "system" may be partially glimpsed in the anecdotal moments of apparent excess that reveal its unstated norms and laws. The places at which breakdown and grotesquerie manifest themselves are precisely the signs of its normal operation, and the only way the subject and vehicle of this system can speak is not in the form of some sequentially satisfying narrative, but through a pile-up of seemingly arbitrary disruptions of "normal" conditions. That is, by complaining about eruptions of its perverse or aberrant experiential effects.

This is why *Woman-Prisoner* can be read superficially as a kind of shrill harangue (though we would argue that shrillness and harangue are quite interesting literary registers in themselves). Indeed, contemporary critical responses to *Woman-Prisoner* laid precisely these kinds of charges against the work.

> One day, just after *Woman-Prisoner* was published, Rokeya said in conversation, "I've heard that some people are saying that many of the incidents in *Woman-Prisoner* are so outlandish they can't believe they truly happened. But I know myself that not a single letter of it exceeds the truth."[28]

---

28 *Rokeya Jībanī*, 115.

It is likely that she was responding to comments such as the following, part of a letter published in the *Monthly Mohammadi* in August 1931: "If, in order to vilify the seclusion-system, the respected authoress had not stooped to making up so many fables [*upakatha*], readers would probably have been better pleased."[29]

We hope it is clear that the denial and disbelief confronting Rokeya in the reception of this work are entirely symptomatic. In staging the outlandish, the excessive, the unbelievable as an infinitely repetitive component of women's normal experience, *Woman-Prisoner* both accommodates and provides a kind of explanation of the disbelief it provoked.

Finally, if in certain ways *Woman-Prisoner's* unrelenting litany of bleakness and despair seems bitter and pessimistic—if darkly humorous—in comparison to Rokeya's other writings, this is partly because the work is a product of many years of difficult and often lonely practical and public struggle.

"TRUE DAWN"

Published in the quarterly journal *Muezzin* in 1930, this piece is among the last of Rokeya's works published in her lifetime. The title is an Arabic phrase lexicalized into Bengali, "sube sadek" (Arabic: subh-i-sadiq). The phrase refers to the moment a new day is held to start in Islamic chronological systems: the true or real dawn, the first visible trace of the sun. With its insistent motifs of awakening, opening one's eyes, coming to consciousness, and rising up, the piece announces itself as a manifesto. And it gives the manifesto-form a brilliant Indo-Islamic idiom in the emblem of the muezzin's call to prayer: "Awake mother, sister, daughter—arise, off your beds, come; advance. Listen here, 'Muezzin' calls out the azan." While a muezzin—literally one who calls—is the person who sings the periodic daily calls to prayer from a mosque, *Muezzin* was also the name of the journal in which Rokeya published this work. Thus the word condenses several meanings in this context: a familiar summons in Islamic practice, the contemporary publication as a calling voice, and Rokeya's own manifesto in this very journal as a call within a call. A call to women by a female muezzin.

---

29   *RR*, 599.

The rhetoric of this manifesto thus stages self-enlightenment as a sacred duty.

Reprising in a brief, terse, and imperative form many of the themes Rokeya was concerned with in the later part of her life, "True Dawn" also resonates with the global atmosphere of revolution, rebellion, and militancy that had intensified during the later 1920s. Disciplined mass movements were everywhere: nationalist, Hindu nationalist or otherwise ethnonationalist, socialist, fascist. Such that while Rokeya's turn to physical discipline, combat, and national service at the end of the piece might seem odd today, it actually catches an aspect of the era's complexity and character. Yet the main object of "True Dawn" is the call for consciousness in the figure of awakening to the light of a new day. Bengali women have fallen behind the times: they "are laying in deep sleep on the dark, damp floors of domestic dungeons and dying of tuberculosis by the thousands" as other women around the world progress. They have so internalized their construction as, in Rokeya's words, "slaves" and "animals" (yet, paradoxically precious ornaments) that their lives are an unconscious reverie of delusion in which oppression is not even registered. In this impossible condition, abjection and veneration seem to add up to the same thing. A manifesto is, of course, only a call. It pleads to be answered in acts. The anger and ferocity almost audible in this piece testify to Rokeya's sense of the forces and energies needed to transform women's minds, desires, and actions.

There is a great deal more to be said and written about Rokeya Sakhawat Hossain. We reserve that for others and for our own future publications. For the time being, we invite the reader to engage with some of the very best of her writings in the pages that follow.

TRANSLATOR'S NOTE

All the translations for this volume are new. I have benefited from consulting previous translations of Rokeya's writings by Roushan Jahan, Kalyani Dutta, Ratri Ray and Prantosh Bandyopadhyay, Barnita Bagchi, and Mohammad A. Quayum. Roushan Jahan is owed a particular debt of gratitude for both pioneering the translation of Rokeya's Bengali writings and introducing me to her work many years ago.

Rokeya's first biographer, Shamsunnahar Mahmud, makes the convincing claim that Rokeya's writing style was a new and original development in Bengali literature. There is a unique modernist poetics emerging in her work that I would argue is strongly determined by the lack of formal education she so often lamented. Rokeya's originality is in part the product of an absence of training in prevailing literary competences and the consequent imperative to invent her own ones.

The majority of Rokeya's literary texts are composed using the inflections of the modernized nineteenth-century "chaste" Bengali (*suddha bhasa*) rather than the stripped-down "colloquial" Bengali (*chalita bhasa*) that became the norm in the twentieth. Nevertheless, they are direct and colloquial in tone except when she is deploying high-register language for a literary effect.

The translations have been made from the *Rokeya Racanabali* (Collected Works of Rokeya), edited by Abdul Kadir (Dhaka: Bangla Akademi, 2021). This is the authoritative edition of her writings. I have also consulted other editions of the *Collected Works* for the sake of consistency and precision.

I have included translator's footnotes where we deemed it necessary to do so. They are indicated each time as a "Translator's note." All other footnotes are Rokeya's own.

—BEN BAER

SULTANA'S DREAM[1]

1 In the text of "Sultana's Dream" we have stayed as close as possible to the original layout, capitalization, and punctuation of the story. We have silently corrected a small number of obvious typographical errors. The dedication to the story was added when "Sultana's Dream" was published as a small book in 1908.

DEDICATION

To my elder sister who was kind enough to help me in my childhood
to commence my ABC of the English language this little book is
reverently dedicated.

One evening I was lounging in an easy chair in my bed-room and thinking lazily of the condition of Indian womanhood. I am not sure whether I dozed off or not. But, as far as I remember, I was wide awake. I saw the moonlit sky sparkling with thousands of diamond-like stars, very distinctly.

All on a sudden a lady stood before me; how she came in, I do not know. I took her for my friend, Sister Sara.

"Good morning," said Sister Sara. I smiled inwardly as I knew it was not morning, but starry night. However, I replied to her, saying, "How do you do?"

"I am all right, thank you. Will you please come out and have a look at our garden?"

I looked again at the moon through the open window, and thought there was no harm in going out at that time. The men-servants outside were fast asleep just then, and I could have a pleasant walk with Sister Sara.

I used to have my walks with Sister Sara, when we were at Darjeeling. Many a time did we walk hand in hand and talk light-heartedly in the botanical gardens there. I fancied, Sister Sara had probably come to take me to some such garden and I readily accepted her offer and went out with her.

When walking I found to my surprise that it was a fine morning. The town was fully awake and the streets alive with bustling crowds. I was feeling very shy, thinking I was walking in the street in broad daylight, but there was not a single man visible.

Some of the passers-by made jokes at me. Though I could not understand their language, yet I felt sure they were joking. I asked my friend, "What do they say?"

"The women say that you look very mannish."

"Mannish?" said I, "What do they mean by that?"

"They mean that you are shy and timid like men."

"Shy and timid like men?" It was really a joke. I became very nervous, when I found that my companion was not Sister Sara, but a stranger.

Oh, what a fool had I been to mistake this lady for my dear old friend, Sister Sara.

She felt my fingers tremble in her hand, as we were walking hand in hand.

"What is the matter, dear?" she said affectionately. "I feel somewhat awkward," I said in a rather apologizing tone, "as being a purdahnishin woman I am not accustomed to walking about unveiled."

"You need not be afraid of coming across a man here. This is Ladyland, free from sin and harm. Virtue herself reigns here."

By and by I was enjoying the scenery. Really it was very grand. I mistook a patch of green grass for a velvet cushion. Feeling as if I were walking on a soft carpet, I looked down and found the path covered with moss and flowers.

"How nice it is," said I.

"Do you like it?" asked Sister Sara. (I continued calling her "Sister Sara," and she kept calling me by my name).

"Yes, very much; but I do not like to tread on the tender and sweet flowers."

"Never mind, dear Sultana; your treading will not harm them; they are street flowers."

"The whole place looks like a garden," said I admiringly. "You have arranged every plant so skillfully."

"Your Calcutta could become a nicer garden than this if only your countrymen wanted to make it so."

"They would think it useless to give so much attention to horticulture, while they have so many other things to do."

"They could not find a better excuse," said she with smile.

I became very curious to know where the men were. I met more than a hundred women while walking there, but not a single man.

"Where are the men?" I asked her.

"In their proper places, where they ought to be."

"Pray let me know what you mean by their proper places."

"O, I see my mistake, you cannot know our customs, as you were never here before. We shut our men indoors."

"Just as we are kept in the zenana?"

"Exactly so."

"How funny," I burst into a laugh. Sister Sara laughed too.

"But dear Sultana, how unfair it is to shut in the harmless women and let loose the men."

"Why? It is not safe for us to come out of the zenana, as we are naturally weak."

"Yes, it is not safe so long as there are men about the streets, nor is it so when a wild animal enters a marketplace."

"Of course not."

"Suppose, some lunatics escape from the asylum and begin to do all sorts of mischief to men, horses and other creatures; in that case what will your countrymen do?"

"They will try to capture them and put them back into their asylum."

"Thank you! And you do not think it wise to keep sane people inside an asylum and let loose the insane?"

"Of course not!" said I laughing lightly.

"As a matter of fact, in your country this very thing is done! Men, who do or at least are capable of doing no end of mischief, are let loose and the innocent women, shut up in the zenana! How can you trust those untrained men out of doors?"

"We have no hand or voice in the management of our social affairs. In India man is lord and master, he has taken to himself all powers and privileges and shut up the women in the zenana."

"Why do you allow yourselves to be shut up?"

"Because it cannot be helped as they are stronger than women."

"A lion is stronger than a man, but it does not enable him to dominate the human race. You have neglected the duty you owe to yourselves and you have lost your natural rights by shutting your eyes to your own interests."

"But my dear Sister Sara, if we do everything by ourselves, what will the men do then?"

"They should not do anything, excuse me; they are fit for nothing. Only catch them and put them into the zenana."

"But would it be very easy to catch and put them inside the four walls?" said I. "And even if this were done, would all their business— political and commercial—also go with them into the zenana?"

Sister Sara made no reply. She only smiled sweetly. Perhaps she thought it useless to argue with one who was no better than a frog in a well.

By this time we reached Sister Sara's house. It was situated in a beautiful heart-shaped garden. It was a bungalow with a corrugated iron roof. It was cooler and nicer than any of our rich buildings. I cannot describe how neat and how nicely furnished and how tastefully decorated it was.

We sat side by side. She brought out of the parlour a piece of embroidery work and began putting on a fresh design.

"Do you know knitting and needle work?"

"Yes; we have nothing else to do in our zenana."

"But we do not trust our zenana members with embroidery!" she said laughing, "as a man has not patience enough to pass thread through a needlehole even!"

"Have you done all this work yourself?" I asked her pointing to the various pieces of embroidered teapoy cloths.

"Yes."

"How can you find time to do all these? You have to do the office work as well? Have you not?"

"Yes. I do not stick to the laboratory all day long. I finish my work in two hours."

"In two hours! How do you manage? In our land the officers,— magistrates, for instance, work seven hours daily."

"I have seen some of them doing their work. Do you think they work all the seven hours?"

"Certainly they do!"

"No, dear Sultana, they do not. They dawdle away their time in smoking. Some smoke two or three choroots during the office time. They talk much about their work, but do little. Suppose one choroot takes half an hour to burn off, and a man smokes twelve choroots daily; then you see, he wastes six hours every day in sheer smoking."

We talked on various subjects; and I learned that they were not subject to any kind of epidemic disease,—nor did they suffer from mosquito-bites as we do. I was very much astonished to hear that in Ladyland no one died in youth except by rare accident.

"Will you care to see our kitchen?" she asked me.

"With pleasure," said I, and we went to see it. Of course the men had been asked to clear off when I was going there. The kitchen was situated in a beautiful vegetable garden. Every creeper, every tomato plant was itself an ornament. I found no smoke, nor any chimney either in the kitchen,—it was clean and bright; the windows were decorated with flower gardens. There was no sign of coal or fire.

"How do you cook?" I asked.

"With solar heat," she said, at the same time showing me the pipe, through which passed the concentrated sunlight and heat. And she cooked something then and there to show me the process.

"How did you manage to gather and store up the sun-heat?" I asked her in amazement.

"Let me tell you a little of our past history then. Thirty years ago, when our present Queen was thirteen years old, she inherited the throne. She was Queen in name only, the Prime-Minister really ruling the country.

"Our good Queen liked science very much. She circulated an order that all the women in her country should be educated. Accordingly a number of girls' schools were founded and supported by the government. Education was spread far and wide among women. And early marriage also was stopped. No woman was to be allowed to marry before she was twenty-one. I must tell you that, before this change we had been kept in strict-purdah."

"How the tables are turned," I interposed with a laugh.

"But the seclusion is the same," she said. "In a few years we had separate universities, where no men were admitted."

"In the capital, where our Queen lives, there are two Universities. One of these invented a wonderful balloon, to which they attached a number of pipes. By means of this captive balloon which they managed to keep afloat above the cloud-land, they could draw as much water from the atmosphere as they pleased. As the water was incessantly being drawn by the University people no cloud gathered and the ingenious Lady Principal stopped rain and storms thereby."

"Really! Now I understand why there is no mud here!" said I. But I could not understand how it was possible to accumulate water in the pipes. She explained to me how it was done; but I was unable to understand her, as my scientific knowledge was very limited. However, she went on,—"When the other University came to know of this, they became exceedingly jealous and tried to do something more extraordinary still. They invented an instrument by which they could collect as much sun-heat as they wanted. And they kept the heat stored up to be distributed among others as required.

"While the women were engaged in scientific research, the men of this country were busy increasing their military power. When they came to know that the female Universities were able to draw water from the atmosphere and collect heat from the sun, they only laughed at the members of the Universities and called the whole thing 'a sentimental nightmare'!"

"Your achievements are very wonderful indeed! But tell me, how you managed to put the men of your country into the zenana. Did you entrap them first?"

"No."

"It is not likely that they would surrender their free and open air life of their own accord and confine themselves within the four walls of the zenana! They must have been overpowered."

"Yes, they have been!"

"By whom? By some lady-warriors, I suppose?"

"No, not by arms."

"Yes, it cannot be so. Men's arms are stronger than women's. Then?"

"By brain."

"Even their brains are bigger and heavier than women's. Are they not?"

"Yes, but what of that? An elephant also has got a bigger and heavier brain than a man has. Yet man can enchain elephants and employ them, according to their own wishes."

"Well said, but tell me please, how it all actually happened. I am dying to know it!"

"Women's brains are somewhat quicker than men's. Ten years ago, when the military officers called our scientific discoveries 'a sentimental nightmare,' some of the young ladies wanted to say something in reply to those remarks. But both the Lady Principals restrained them and said, they should reply, not by word, but by deed, if ever they got the opportunity. And they had not long to wait for that opportunity."

"How marvelous!" I heartily clapped my hands. "And now the proud gentlemen are dreaming sentimental dreams themselves."

"Soon afterwards certain persons came from a neighbouring country and took shelter in ours. They were in trouble having committed some political offense. The king who cared more for power than for good government asked our kind-hearted Queen to hand them over to his officers. She refused, as it was against her principle to turn out refugees. For this refusal the king declared war against our country.

"Our military officers sprang to their feet at once and marched out to meet the enemy.

"The enemy however, was too strong for them. Our soldiers fought bravely, no doubt. But in spite of all their bravery the foreign army advanced step by step to invade our country.

"Nearly all the men had gone out to fight; even a boy of sixteen was not left home. Most of our warriors were killed, the rest driven back and the enemy came within twenty-five miles of the capital.

"A meeting of a number of wise ladies was held at the Queen's palace to advise as to what should be done to save the land.

"Some proposed to fight like soldiers; others objected and said that women were not trained to fight with swords and guns, nor were they accustomed to fighting with any weapons. A third party regretfully remarked that they were hopelessly weak of body.

"If you cannot save your country for lack of physical strength," said the Queen, "try to do so by brain power."

"There was a dead silence for a few minutes. Her Royal Highness said again, 'I must commit suicide if the land and my honour are lost.'

"Then the Lady Principal of the second University (who had collected sun-heat), who had been silently thinking during the consultation, remarked that they were all but lost; and there was little hope left for them. There was, however, one plan which she would like to try, and this would be her first and last efforts; if she failed in this, there would be nothing left but to commit suicide. All present solemnly vowed that they would never allow themselves to be enslaved, no matter what happened.

"The Queen thanked them heartily, and asked the Lady Principal to try her plan.

"The Lady Principal rose again and said, 'before we go out the men must enter the zenanas. I make this prayer for the sake of purdah.' 'Yes, of course,' replied Her Royal Highness.

"On the following day the Queen called upon all men to retire into zenanas for the sake of honour and liberty.

"Wounded and tired as they were, they took that order rather for a boon! They bowed low and entered the zenanas without uttering a single word of protest. They were sure that there was no hope for this country at all.

"Then the Lady Principal with her two thousand students marched to the battle-field, and arriving there directed all the rays of the concentrated sunlight and heat towards the enemy.

"The heat and light were too much for them to bear. They all ran away panic-stricken, not knowing in their bewilderment how to counteract that scorching heat. When they fled away leaving their guns and other ammunitions of war, they were burnt down by means of the same sun-heat.

"Since then no one has tried to invade our country any more."

"And since then your country-men never tried to come out of the zenana?"

"Yes, they wanted to be free. Some of the Police Commissioners and District Magistrates sent word to the Queen to the effect that the Military Officers certainly deserved to be imprisoned for their failure; but they never neglected their duty and therefore they should not be punished and they prayed to be restored to their respective offices.

"Her Royal Highness sent them a circular letter intimating to them that if their services should ever be needed they would be sent for, and that in the meanwhile they should remain where they were.

"Now that they are accustomed to the purdah system and have ceased to grumble at their seclusion, we call the system 'Murdana' instead of 'zenana.'"

"But how do you manage," I asked Sister Sara, "to do without the Police or Magistrates in case of theft or murder?"

"Since the 'Murdana' system has been established, there has been no more crime or sin; therefore we do not require a Police-man to find out a culprit, nor do we want a Magistrate to try a criminal case."

"That is very good, indeed. I suppose if there was any dishonest person, you could very easily chastise her. As you gained a decisive victory without shedding a single drop of blood, you could drive off crime and criminals too without much difficulty!"

"Now, dear Sultana, will you sit here or come to my parlour?" she asked me.

"Your kitchen is not inferior to a queen's boudoir!" I replied with a pleasant smile, "but we must leave it now; for the gentlemen may be cursing me for keeping them away from their duties in the kitchen so long." We both laughed heartily.

"How my friends at home will be amused and amazed, when I go back and tell them that in the far-off Ladyland, ladies rule over the country and control all social matters, while gentlemen are kept in the Murdanas to mind babies, to cook and to do all sorts of domestic work; and that cooking is so easy a thing that it is simply a pleasure to cook!"

"Yes, tell them about all that you see here."

"Please let me know, how you carry on land cultivation and how you plough the land and do other hard manual work."

"Our fields are tilled by means of electricity, which supplies motive power for other hard work as well, and we employ it for our aerial conveyances too. We have no rail road nor any paved streets here."

"Therefore neither street nor railway accidents occur here," said I. "Do not you ever suffer from want of rainwater?" I asked.

"Never since the 'water balloon' has been set up. You see the big balloon and pipes attached thereto. By their aid we can draw as much rainwater as we require. Nor do we ever suffer from flood or thunderstorms. We are all very busy making nature yield as much as she can. We do not find time to quarrel with one another as we never sit idle. Our noble Queen is exceedingly fond of botany; it is her ambition to convert the whole country into one grand garden."

"The idea is excellent. What is your chief food?"

"Fruits."

"How do you keep your country cool in hot weather? We regard the rainfall in summer as a blessing from heaven."

"When the heat becomes unbearable, we sprinkle the ground with plentiful showers drawn from the artificial fountains. And in cold weather we keep our room warm with sun-heat."

She showed me her bathroom, the roof of which was removable. She could enjoy a shower bath whenever she liked, by simply removing the roof (which was like the lid of a box) and turning on the tap of the shower pipe.

"You are a lucky people!" ejaculated I. "You know no want. What is your religion, may I ask?"

"Our religion is based on Love and Truth. It is our religious duty to love one another and to be absolutely truthful. If any person lies, she or he is——"

"Punished with death?"

"No; not with death. We do not take pleasure in killing a creature of God,—specially a human being. The liar is asked to leave this land for good and never to come to it again."

"Is an offender never forgiven?"

"Yes, if that person repents sincerely."

"Are you not allowed to see any man, except your own relations?"

"No one except sacred relations."

"Our circle of sacred relations is very limited too, even first cousins are not sacred."

"But ours is very large; a distant cousin is as sacred as a brother."

"That is very good. I see purity itself reigns over your land. I should like to see the good Queen, who is so sagacious and far-sighted and who has made all these rules."

"All right," said Sister Sara.

Then she screwed a couple of seats onto a square piece of plank. To this plank she attached two smooth and well-polished balls. When I asked her what the balls were for, she said, they were hydrogen balls and they were used to overcome the force of gravity. The balls were of different capacities to be used according to the different weights desired to be overcome. She then fastened to the air-car two wing-like blades, which, she said, were worked by electricity. After we were comfortably seated she touched a knob and the blades began to whirl, moving faster and faster every moment. At first we were raised to the height of about six or seven feet and then off we flew. And before I could realize that we had commenced moving, we reached the Garden of the Queen.

My friend lowered the air-car by reversing the action of the machine, and when the car touched the ground the machine was stopped and we got out.

I had seen from the air-car the Queen walking on a garden path with her little daughter (who was four years old) and her maids of honour.

"Hallo! You here!" cried the Queen addressing Sister Sara. I was introduced to Her Royal Highness and was received by her cordially without any ceremony.

I was very much delighted to make her acquaintance. In the course of the conversation I had with her, the Queen told me that she had no objection to permitting her subjects to trade with other countries. "But," she continued, "no trade was possible with countries where the women were kept in the zenanas and so unable to come and trade with us. Men, we find, are rather of lower morals and so we do not like dealing with them. We do not covet other people's land, we do not fight for a piece of diamond though it may be a thousand-fold brighter than the Koh-i-Noor, nor do we grudge a ruler his Peacock Throne. We dive deep into the ocean of knowledge and try to find out the precious gems, which nature has kept in store for us. We enjoy nature's gifts as much as we can."

After taking leave of the Queen, I visited the famous Universities, and was shown some of their manufactories, laboratories, and observatories.

After visiting the above places of interest we got again into the air-car, but as soon as it began moving, I somehow slipped down and the fall startled me out of my dream. And on opening my eyes, I found myself in my own bedroom still lounging in the easy-chair!!

THE CONDITION OF WOMANHOOD

JUSTICE IS VIRTUE

SULTANA UNIVERSITY

WATER STORAGE

ORACLE IN THE BAOLI

SOLAR HANDS

ART OF WAR 1

OVER THE CITY

FIFTY MILES IN AN AIRPLANE
(DREAM FULFILLED)

It was a long time ago (1905). We were then in a subdivision of Bhagalpur called Banka. The late Deputy Saheb (my revered husband) went on a tour of the district; I was completely alone at home. To pass the time, I wrote a bit. When he returned two days later he asked me what I had been doing! In reply I showed him a written draft, "Sultana's Dream." Still standing there, he read the whole thing and exclaimed—"A Terrible Revenge."[1] Thereafter, he sent the composition to the then Commissioner, Mr. MacPherson, for revisions.

When, in due course, I got the text back from Mr. MacPherson I saw that he had not made a single written mark on it. It was accompanied by a letter to the Deputy Saheb, and this is what it said:

"The ideas expressed in it are quite delightful and full of originality and they are written in perfect English...I wonder if she has foretold here the manner in which we may be able to move about in the air at some future time. Her suggestions on this point are most ingenious."[2]

At the time I wrote "Sultana's Dream," there were no airplanes or zeppelins in existence; motorcars had not even reached India yet. Electric lights and fans existed in an imaginary future. I, at least, had never seen any of this at that time.

About six years later (in 1911) when I came to Calcutta, I saw my first airplane rising into the void. I never entertained the hope that I would myself be able to board an airplane. I merely gasped in silence.

Last November 31 (1930), at the end of Sunday evening, Sriman

---

1 Translator's note: "A Terrible Revenge" (capitalized in original) appears in English type followed by a parenthetical translation of the phrase into Bengali: "(bhayankar pratishodh!)."

2 Translator's note: This paragraph is in English type in the original. It is followed by a Bengali translation of the same which we have not re-translated here.

Murad arrived and said, "Aunt, come along, I'm going to take you up in my plane the day after tomorrow; it'll take about thirty-five minutes to fly all the way around Calcutta!" My heart leaped with an unprecedented joy. I did not tell this wonderful news to many people for two reasons: The first was that two months previously the large airplane "R 101" had crashed and forty-five luckless passengers had been sent bodily to hell. People would have stopped me going up because the terrible memory of this was still vivid in their minds, and airplanes were a thing of dread and horror. The second reason was that many would have shown up with cameras to take my photograph.

We made the happy journey at the appointed time, on Tuesday, December 2, around four in the afternoon. Mrs. Rashad (Sriman Murad's mother), her third son Foyad, Mrs. De, and I were in one car; my sister and her son and daughter were in the other car. On the way, I saw that beloved sister Mrs. Daudar Rahman was there, too. She was also accompanying us to Dumdum.

Once we got to the aerodrome, I saw a completely open field! Just our three cars and ourselves! I gave thanks to God and got into the plane of the pride of Bengal, its first Muslim pilot, Sriman Murad. On ascending into the sky I see—the earth really is curved like a bowl. I gradually climbed to an altitude of 3,000 feet. Then the view was really amazing. To my right the setting sun, to my left the almost-full moon of the eleventh day of the month of Rajab (twelfth day of the lunar fortnight)—as if they were looking at me from each side and softly smiling. I look down and see—Calcutta's brick houses, multi-stories, districts, it all resembled little piles of bricks—Howrah Bridge like some diminutive kind of toy, and the Hooghly River—it looked like a tiny line of water. We circled fifty miles and descended. After I got down, Mrs. Rashad flew for five minutes. Thanks be to God.[3]

I had really traveled in the air as I had described twenty-five years earlier in "Sultana's Dream." It was me: I was the first woman-prisoner to have flown with Bengal's first Muslim pilot. However many Muslim women got in an airplane after me, they all flew with skilled European pilots. And they had helmets on their heads, earphones on their ears, and goggles over their eyes. I had none of this. I went in a completely

---

3   Translator's note; Rokeya here gives the Arabic/Urdu thanks to God: "Shukar alhamdulillah."

defenseless, powerless state with a young man. There was no way at all I could have spoken to Murad during the trip if I had needed to. Not having learned that the cold would be uncomfortable, I handed over my shawl to Mrs. De. When we sat in the plane, Murad said, "Aunt! It would be good to cover your ears." Pfft. What am I supposed to cover my ears with?—I had gotten rid of the shawl. At that point, my only resource was the hood of my sari. I understood why Murad had told me to cover my ears when the engine's terrifying roar deafened me. But the pain, unbearable though it was, felt insignificant in comparison with the outpouring of my inner joy.

Air-hero Murad's true courage is highly praiseworthy. It is our heartfelt prayer that God grants his wish and brings him back safely.

But I say this: Mrs. Rashad does not lack endurance and courage. It is a wonder how this poor, helpless widow, with so much weight to carry, allowed her first son to set off for Cape Town all alone and has now also allowed Murad to go alone to England to learn how to work on airplanes. May God be her support! Amen!

FRUIT OF KNOWLEDGE[1]

(A FABLE)

---

1 I have not here followed the events as described in the Holy Quran or the Bible.

A dam and Eve once lived in the Garden of Eden.[2] As guests of the Lord God they were in utmost comfort and bliss; they lacked nothing! God had prohibited Adam and his wife from eating the fruit of just one tree.

One day as Eve was going along the saffron-bedded paths of the heavenly garden she lay down in the shade of that forbidden tree. She gazed at the beauty of the grove with enchanted eyes. Listening to the sweet sounds of birds in the trees, she unthinkingly plucked some fruit and consumed a piece.

The eyes of Eve's knowledge opened wide as soon as she partook of the fruit. Then she could understand that, while they lived like royalty as guests of the King, she was nonetheless in such a state that she did not even have a shred of cloth upon her exquisite limbs. She instantly spread her knee-length tresses over her body. Some new kind of inner torment assailed her heart with a burden of sorrow.

Just then, Adam presented himself. Eve implored him to eat the fruit in her hands. Adam's knowledge, too, awakened as he consumed his wife's remaining fruit of knowledge. With a heavy heart, he began to be conscious of his wretched state. —Is this really paradise? A loveless, workless, listless life—is this heavenly bliss? He understood more: he is the Lord's captive; he has not the power to step beyond the borders of this Garden of Eden! He lives in a gorgeous palace of gold and silver bricks that are held together (in place of mortar) with powdered coral and pearl, yet there is not one thing he can call "mine"—not even a single scrap of clothing! What kind of regal luxury is this? Now the unconscious dream of heavenly pleasures shattered—knowledge awakened brought clear perception! And so in place of ignorance and calm, awareness and disturbance disclosed themselves! To Eve he said, "We've been deluded for so long! How happy we were like that!"

Eve replied, "Just so! This lovely, most-favored land—bedded with verdure of fragrant saffron-flowers; these graceful,

<hr />

2 Translator's note: in her text, Rokeya uses the more Hebraic/Arabic word "Habha/Hava" for the name here Anglicized as "Eve."

diamond-flower-dressed vines; these great emerald-leaf-embellished treetops with ruby fruits—of course they delight the eye, but how do they satisfy life's longings? Of course, the nectar-like waters of Lake Kosar quench the need to drink, but how do they satisfy the heart's thirst? What use are all these heavenly riches to us?" They were consumed by the unknown possibility of some kind of transformation.

God visited the garden and noticed that Adam and his wife hid themselves behind a tree upon seeing him. The Lord called to them, but from resentment, disgrace, shame, they could not approach the divine being. The all-knowing Almighty understood everything; enraged, he said, "Want independence, do you? Then go, get lost! Go to earth and see how lovely independence is!"

Adam and his wife fell to earth that very day. Here they endured many trials of lightness and dark, scarcity and comfort, grief-joy-sickness, health, good times and bad, accomplishing the real life of a couple! Eve loves her daughters intensely, makes her female line live long, sets them up in happy, peaceful homes; amasses an indestructible store of love in their hearts.

Adam, too, cared for his sons deeply, but his willpower had no such strength and he did not give his sons any special gifts.

With mother Eve's blessings, her clutch of daughters, once born, grew twice as strong, lived four times longer! And Adam's favorite sons, once born, raised too indulgently, were twice as susceptible to sickness and four times more likely to die! When they did not die naturally, they killed each other fighting in wars and battles! They rotted away in prisons and suffered many torments!

Banished from paradise, Eve tossed her half-eaten fruit of knowledge down to earth. From its seed a great tree was born in the east of the world. In time, the tree bloomed and fruit swelled; but in those days, the people of that land did not know how to tend it properly. Pile upon pile of ripe fruit lay fallen at the base of the tree, jackals and crows filled their bellies. The remaining fruit heaped up near the banks of the Shanta river; some of it rolled right into the stream!

In time, river water mixed with juices of the fruit of knowledge flowed down to the great ocean and blended with it. On the other side of the great ocean was Faerieland.[3]

---

3 Translator's note: "Faerieland" translates "Parīsthan" from the Bengali noun

The people of Faerieland looked really beautiful, but apart from their physical beauty there was nothing special about them to boast of. This land only had forests of makal fruit.[4] A severe shortage of sufficient food. The jinn-folk,[5] despite their inventiveness, hard labor and toil, could not work this harsh, infertile soil to the point where it would bear sufficient fruits. The faerie-folk lived in heavenlike luxury, surrounded by all manner of lavish things; they are extremely wealthy for sure, but they burn with starvation! How providence plays its surprising tricks!

One day at bathing time a few of the jinns, driven over the edge by hunger, swallowed some of the great ocean's salty water. As soon as they drank the water, the veil of their ignorance was lifted. All this time they had not been able to solve that intricate and troubling problem of food supply; now the solution had become simple. The miracle of knowledge was able to show them the way.

That day, the jinn-folk made up their minds: they would travel to other countries and be merchants. Henceforth, they loaded up ships with makal fruit and set forth in the business of trade. After passing close by many lands, they arrived at harbor in Golden Island on the other side of the great ocean! A race of golden people lived on Golden Island.

The jinn merchants were transfixed by the sight of the flourishing cities of Golden Island. They had thought there was no land as wealthy as their own, that "the dirt they touched turned to gold"! But the soil of Golden Island births treasures! Here there are many species of trees with delicious fruit, among which groves of mango predominate. The highly civilized, saintly natured people of this place live mainly by consuming fruit. The jinn merchants thought: There should be some

---

"pari" meaning a female winged, sylph-like (apsara-like) supernatural being, and "sthan" (place, land).

4   Translator's note: Makal is a fruit-bearing climbing plant fairly common in Eastern India (and Bangladesh). The fruit is highly attractive to look at but foul tasting and virtually inedible. Its established cultural significance is as a metaphor for something that looks tempting on the outside but is useless and unpleasant on the inside.

5   Jinn—male. Faerie—female.
Translator's addition: Jinn can be rendered as djinn, genie: a noun lexicalized from the Arabic for a (usually, but not exclusively, masculine) powerful spirit. Pari, as noted previously, is a name for a female fairy or winged nymph.

way we can swindle them. Then they went to the people of Golden Island and made exchanges of makal for sonamukhi mangoes, andharmanik mangoes, and so on. In this way, every year, ships loaded with makal would arrive and mango-filled ships would depart. The trade gradually grew larger. But to the wonderful growth of their trade, there corresponded a mango-famine on Golden Island.

The next year, the merchants were troubled to see a lack of mangoes in the markets. Leaving the cities, they went out to the villages in search of mangoes. In the villages they saw field upon field overflowing with golden autumn rice! With joy in their hearts, the farmers were carrying bale after bale of rice to their homes. The jinns let out a deep sigh at this sight—"They don't know the torment of starvation!" After some vacillation, the merchants approached the farmers and requested that they exchange rice for makal. The farmers did not understand their language; and besides, a group of plump and merry little children surrounded the jinns in wonder. They stared with intense curiosity at the lovely visages of the jinns, looking very closely! The merchants thought to themselves, "What's this mockery! We've been turned into entertainment for farmers' kids!"

In any case, the merchants were somehow able to make their intentions known to a farmer. At first the farmer refused to give rice in exchange for makal; but his son said, "Oh! Give, they are hungry. We have so much rice!"[6]

The number of merchant ships began to grow by the year in intellectually and scientifically developed Faerieland. There was now no threat of famine or shortage, so the faerie-folk no longer suffered in any way. Whenever they felt like it, they would travel on their magical chariots to Golden Island. The female inhabitants of Golden Island became very close to them. As a result, they began making great efforts to imitate the outfits of the faerie-folk. The only thing left to copy was the faerie-folks' pairs of wings!

Previously, one or two ships per year had come to import makal; later, numberless boatloads of makal began arriving in Golden Island several times a year. And enormous amounts of rice were exported to Faerieland. Makal cast such a spell that the farmers could no longer

---

6   Alas!—"To other folk you sell your rice
In return famine's your price!"

restrain themselves. And the farmers no longer stored rice for a year; what gradually happened was that whatever could be cut and collected from the paddy field today could tomorrow be sold in exchange for makal. Thus did the demon-queen of famine come and make her home on Golden Island.

A noteworthy incident occurred at the time of the makal-trade. A stupendous guava tree had sprung up on the shores of the great ocean. Sustained by water mixed with juices of the fruit of knowledge, these guavas had a little of that fruit's quality. The jinn- and faerie-folk would carefully gather these guavas and save them for themselves. But one day as the merchants were loading their ships with makal, a number of guavas fell from the treetop into a ship. These guavas were brought to Golden Island and sold along with the makal.

A few lucky folk of Golden Island ate the guavas that had come from Faerieland and tossed away the seeds. From those seeds, a guava tree grew on Golden Island, too. A hundred years slowly passed.

*   *   *

Helped by guava fruit, a number of Golden Island's gentlefolk awoke from their deluded reveries! After so long—after centuries of unwitting slumber—what a harsh awakening it was! The blind regained sight only to be plunged into deepest darkness! They looked around in wide-eyed amazement and saw that the jinn-folk had taken everything from the land in exchange for a single kind of fruit; now, like leeches, the jinn-folk were sucking out whatever blood was left! Their hearts were torn apart at the wretchedness of Golden Island.

No more mango orchards; no more sweet fruits on the trees; no golden grains in the fields; earth's wealth-filled womb turned to a belly of dust. In every home sounds the agonized cry, "Need food, need food!"; the farmers no longer sleek and well-nourished; their bodies skeletal; clothing patched and torn! The inhabitants of Golden Island have nothing left, just makal and more makal. The shops lining the cities' main streets have only makal for sale; in every village, market, bazaar: makal—the whole land is covered in makal! What to do?

Golden Island's accursed cloud had a silver lining: along with makal, the inhabitants had received the guavas of knowledge and it was therefore not long before they thought of a solution. They vowed no longer to accept makal. As one, each of them took the solemn oath, they will be fooled no more by makal's mirage. Now they were full of a new enthusiasm, they gained a mighty strength—something they would not have been able to obtain so fast if they had not been sapped like this by makal. So with gratitude in their hearts, they offered hundredfold thanks to the jinns.

Meanwhile, the jinn merchants loaded up their ships with makal and arrived at the port as usual. But this time there was no selling of makal. When the traders were unable to sell a single piece of merchandise on these shores, and pile on pile of lovely looking makal started to rot away, they had no recourse but to convey this bad news back to Faerieland!

This matter threw Faerieland's commercial associations into chaos—the turmoil even churned the deep, calm waters of the great ocean! Finally, a rotten-toothed, white-haired old man said, "Go and find out why Golden Island will no longer take makal."

A band of merchants traveled all over Golden Island, heard various accounts, and learned that those who had tasted the guavas were enemies of makal. In the blink of an eye, the traders sent this news by sorcery to Faerieland. That very day, the chief merchant gave an order, "Dig up their guava tree by the roots."

The merchants replied to the chief by sorcery with the following report: "Impossible to dig up such a huge tree by the roots. So what do you command?" The chief merchant immediately decreed: "Cut out its roots!"

The blows of innumerable sharpened axes rained down upon the guava tree's roots. At first, the inhabitants of Golden Island were speechless at the sight; then they understood what this was about! To start with, they implored the jinn-merchants to stop cutting the tree—then they fell and wept at the traders' feet to prevent them. But the jinns were unrelenting. Now Golden Island erupted in terrifying disorder, all across this peaceful land the fires of unrest burned! Yet the jinns were unyielding! Instead they tried to make the golden folk understand:

"Since God prohibited the fruit of knowledge to humans, and the primal mother was expelled from paradise for the sin of eating it, then you must also realize that this fruit is very unsafe for humans. This is why we are doing you a great favor working so hard to cut the tree."

The people of this land were now wise and smart enough not to be deceived by hollow arguments! They said, "But why do you eat that fruit? Cut down Faerieland's tree first and then cut ours. And if the primal mother counted heavenly bliss as nothing beside this fruit, then it is simple to figure out how much the fruit must be worth. Fruit brought from heaven to earth must be preserved with utmost care." But who could hear this?—There's the rub!

For a while, the golden folk debated the cutting of the tree in minute detail. During this time an octogenarian scholar spoke: "Why are you making such a huge fuss over this monstrous guava tree? Its fruit is merely a pale imitation of the primordial fruit of knowledge. Go seek out the primal tree sown by Eve. Scripture tells us that it lies in the east of the world. Come, let us seek it out." In accordance with the old man's words, everyone quit the present in search of the past! The elderly scholar did not go with them, however—having given his advice, his mind was at rest.

After long journeys across vast rivers, human settlements, mountains, plains, forests, the golden folk drew close to the site of a huge dead tree. They perused much scripture, listened to many legends, and finally reached the conclusion that this desiccated trunk was the primordial tree of knowledge. Their chests were rent with agonizing pain, grief, disappointment! Had they come to this land with such effort, far from home, sleeping little, suffering much, for this dead tree? The local folk said that the tree had died almost two centuries ago. One of the arrivals replied, "Well, one good thing is that you have mercifully refrained from offering it up as fuel for your ovens. So it's saved!"

What to do now? How can the tree of knowledge be brought back to life? Some said water it as much as we can; some said moisten it with tears; some said give our hearts' blood. Various proposals like this came up. They were not even afraid of exchanging one or two human lives for the sake of reviving the tree.

Everyone began taking care of the dried-up tree in various ways— none shrank from offering tears or blood! But do the dead ever come back to life? Realizing that all their exertions were futile, they began all manner of heartbroken lamentations. One of them, exhausted by the fierce sun, lay down among the tree roots. He slept, and in his dream appeared a hermit speaking thus:

"My boy! No use weeping. Not just one or two, not even two thousand human sacrifices will restore life to the tree of knowledge. It is two hundred years since the blinkered, selfish scholar-fools of this land prohibited women from partaking in the fruit of knowledge. In due course this prohibition was taken as a social law and the men monopolized this fruit for themselves. The great masses of women forbidden to gather and eat the fruit turned away from nurturing the tree. Without the tender care of women's hands, the tree gradually died! Leave, go back to your land; go plant the seed of this guava. Let the jinn-folk cut whatever tree they want to. Don't stop them, store up the seed in secret. Then let your men and women together tend the new-planted guava saplings; if you do this, you will receive the kind of fruit you hope for. Beware! Do not deprive the female kind of the guava! Women have every right to the fruit of knowledge brought by woman. Hold this in your memory without fail!" On awakening, he recounted the dream to his companions; when they heard it they spoke with one voice: come, let us return. A bighearted gentleman spoke: "That's right. Some men made a deal to cross a river on a crocodile's back and then cheated it—women have been denied the knowledge a woman brought—the result is obvious!"

The enthused young men of Golden Island cleared and marked out a corner of the grove and summoned the young women: "Come, sisters! Join us. With spades we prepare the earth; sow the seed with your hands! This is a blessed day. From now we will have our own tree." The jinns stood silently watching, transfixed with amazement; they could not prevent this hallowed labor. Let the jinns stay away from this grand task performed by the revitalized golden folk with renewed enthusiasm—even demons are powerless to stop it!

Thenceforth Golden Island was once more doubly and trebly replete with prosperity; its inhabitants passed the time in utmost happiness. They will not be misled by any more deception! Because now women are guardians of the garden of knowledge.

The fable of Golden Isle is like nectar,
If the dead hear it, they will come to life.

BURKA

have often heard that it is our "obscene system of seclusion" that obstructs our development. When I meet with highly educated sisters face-to-face, they often tell me to give up the "burka." But what is this thing we call development? Does it dwell only outside the burka? If that is the case, then are we to understand that fishwives, hide-tanners, and corpse-clearers are more developed than us?[1]

Yet it is our belief that there is no excessive conflict between seclusion and development. A high level of education is of course necessary for development. Some say that a high level of education necessarily requires relinquishing purdah and attending a university for F.A. or B.A. examinations. This is not such bad reasoning. Why? Is it impossible for there to be a self-governed university and women examiners for us? We can still keep going even if there is no such arrangement and no knowledge that earns a grade.

The system of seclusion is not natural—it is ethical. Animals do not have this rule. As humankind gradually became civilized, it learned many non-natural practices. For instance: it is natural to travel on foot, but mankind has produced various types of wagons, palanquins, and suchlike for the advantage of human transportation. It is natural to swim across a pond, but mankind has produced all sorts of watercraft. With their aid, even those who cannot swim may traverse the great oceans. The women's inner quarters are themselves a product of the results of this "non-natural" human civilization.

The uncivilized peoples of the world live in a semi-naked state. We

---

1 Translator's note: throughout the essay I translate the Bengali word *abarodh* by "seclusion." I have more forcefully rendered *abarodh* as "prison" or "imprisonment" in Rokeya's later "Woman-Prisoner" included in this volume. The terminological difference, which honors the semantic field of the word, makes "seclusion" more resonant with her argument in the present text composed a quarter-century before "Woman-Prisoner." That is, the ethics, practices, norms, and limits of covering should be considered in a broad cultural and social framework of development.

In the final sentence of this paragraph, Rokeya uses the feminized names of three "untouchable" (Dalit) groups: *jele*, *chamar*, and *dom*, each respectively associated with the occupations of fishing, tanning animal hides, and attending to the bodies of the dead.

learn from history that in the past the uncivilized Britons lived in a semi-naked state. Prior to this semi-naked state, they daubed their bodies with paint! As they gradually became civilized, they learned the usage of clothing.

Now, vaingloriously civilized European ladies and Brahmo Samaj sisters go all over the place entirely covered up except for their faces.[2] And the Muslims of various countries (when they go outside the home) have brought to this mode of covering a full (perfect) development by adding one more cloth screen (burka) for the face itself![3] Those who do not use the burka cover their heads with a veil.

Some object to the burka by calling it heavy. But comparison has revealed that our burka is no heavier than the gigantic hats worn by Englishwomen.

For us, purdah signifies that which is undisclosed, a covered body, et cetera—not just remaining within the four walls of women's quarters. And we call insufficient covering of the body "be-purdah."[4] There are women who appear before their maidservants in a semi-naked state indoors. By contrast, when they depart fully clothed outdoors, to the marketplace, they observe correct purdah.

In the present era, our European sisters have ascended to the very limits of civilization; who can say they do not have purdah? No one can enter their bedchambers or even their sitting rooms without permission. Is this a reprehensible system? Of course not. But unlike Europeans, the sisters of this country who relinquish purdah to imitate English civilization have neither a personal bedchamber (bedroom privacy) nor the burka like us![5]

---

2   Translator's note: the Brahmo Samaj (which still exists today) was a nineteenth-century Hindu "reform" movement. Broadly speaking, it constructed a monotheistic, rationalized, liberal-humanist spiritual institution and practice contesting the prevailing authority of scripture, caste division, and idolatry. Incorporating aspects of the Abrahamic religions as part of its self-styled modernizing endeavor, the Brahmo Samaj and Brahmoism exercised a profound influence upon middle-class intellectual, social, and cultural life in nineteenth- and early twentieth-century Bengal.

3   Translator's note: the word "perfect" appears in English typeface in the original's parenthesis.

4   Translator's note: non-purdah, exposure.

5   Translator's note: the parenthetic phrase "bedroom privacy" appears in English type in the original.

Some have said, "As anyone who has seen it knows, it is a ridiculous thing to cover a lovely body from head to toe with a hideous kind of veil such as the burka and dress up like some bizarre being"—and so on! That's right! But it is our belief that no respectable woman wishes to attract hordes of gawkers as she waits on a railway platform. Therefore it is no loss if we arouse the contempt of onlookers by dressing as an unsightly creature. Well-bred womenfolk will instead think it discreditable to attract crowds of public spectators with the sight of a lovely face.

English conventions of decorum (etiquette) teach us this: that gentlewomen should wear unostentatious (simple) clothing.[6] In particular, when out walking on foot they ought not to wear dazzlingly glamorous outfits.[7]

If going out to keep an invitation, etc., womenfolk usually make use of their most excellent outfits and precious jewelry. A plain (simple) burka is essential to keep those lovely garments hidden from the sight of coachmen, footmen, and others when disembarking the carriage. If traveling by train, a veil or a burka is necessary to protect oneself from the public gaze.

From time to time my European sisters also ask me, "Why don't you break off purdah?"[8] So annoying! Can humanity actually give up purdah? They understand purdah merely to signify staying in the inner quarters. If they only realized that they themselves cannot do without purdah (i.e. privacy) then they would never talk like this.[9] Their clothing clearly does not completely observe purdah—the evening-dresses are especially objectionable. Yet this is still better than the one insubstantial sari so many women wear.

---

6   Translator's note: the parenthetic words appear in English type in the original.
7   In this precept we can hear the echo of a statement in the eighteenth paragraph of Sura Nur in the Holy Quran. Thus—"And say to the believing women, they should ever keep their gaze lowered (that is, not look around hither and thither) let them not display their ornaments to others (except to very specific people)." Translator's addition: in the edition of the Quran I consulted, this quotation is taken from paragraph 31 of Sura Al-Nur (24th Sura). The parenthetic interpolations are Rokeya's.
8   Translator's note: the phrase "Why don't you break off purdah?" appears in parenthesis in English typeface after the synonymous Bengali phrase used by Rokeya.
9   Translator's note: the parenthesis contains the word "privacy" in English type in the original.

Then there is the issue of abandoning the inner quarters—we fail to understand what development there would be in leaving the inner quarters. The aforementioned independent women themselves have another form of inner quarter in the shape of their bedchambers.

In sum, we can see that every civilized people has some form of seclusion-system. What distinction would remain between humans and animals in the absence of a seclusion-system? We cannot comprehend the intention of those who say that such a salutary system of seclusion is "obscene."

Civilization itself has extended purdah in the world. Formerly, people would simply fold their letters and send them off; now they cover their letters with an envelope. Peasants do not cover their rice dishes; by contrast, civilized people put their multiple food containers on a large tray and cover them with a special lid; the yet-more-civilized cover each dish with an individual lid. We could give many more examples of this kind, such as tablecloths, bedcovers, pillowcases, etc.

Our sisters still walk barefoot today, while their own relatives, well-educated (enlightened) sisters, now cover their feet with the shoes and socks of civilization.[10] Gloves were eventually produced to cover the hands. It is thus evident that there is no conflict between civilization and a system of seclusion.

Yet every rule does have its limits. In this country our system of seclusion has become far too harsh. For instance, unmarried girls are compelled to observe purdah even in the company of women! For fear of a female neighbor's imminent visit, a nine-year-old girl cannot go into the yard. Their health is damaged by always being imprisoned like this in some corner of the house. Secondly, the quality of their education is harmed. Since they may not see anyone beside the closest of family relatives, from whom will they learn? The unreasonable purdah of a new bride is also worth mentioning. For the first few months after marriage they are made to live as ornamented "dumb manikins"! Those who have suffered bodily through this kind of artificial blind-mute state will know just what it is like! It is said that once

---

10   Translator's note: the parenthetic word "enlightened" appears in English type in the original. Following Rokeya's implication, I have translated *susiksa, susiksita* (literally: good education, well-educated) as "enlightenment" and "enlightened" hereafter even if she does not insert an English parenthesis.

upon a time the new bride of a well-born family happened to be stung on the back by a scorpion—it was agonizing. She bore it in silence! At the time of the ritual bath on the third day, the other women were dismayed to see the wound on her back! The old women of today make this bride a praiseworthy model! The scorpion was probably not very poisonous!

In any case, all this artificial purdah must be made more moderate. In many families, the womenfolk do not mingle with anyone except their closest kin. Because they are unable to mix with diverse kinds of women, they exist exactly like the famous proverb's frog in a well. It would be good to multiply interactions between inhabitants of the inner quarters. We must continually encounter people of every social class in the way that men do. Of course, we will mix only with those we recognize as courteous and civil—no matter what their professed religion (Jewish, Christian, idol-worshippers or whatever). We really must abandon this observance of purdah with women of "alien faiths." Our religion is not so fragile that it will be destroyed upon contact with women of other religious affiliation—what reason for this kind of fear?

We will relinquish unjust purdah and retain needful purdah. We have no objection to going outdoors in a headcover (aka burka) when necessary. The burka can come with us even when we go to improve our health through excursions in the mountains. Wearing a burka presents no inconvenience for movement. Of course that takes a little practice, but can anything be achieved without practice?

The burka is usually quite coarse in appearance. It will have to be made a bit better-looking (fine). It is urgent to develop the burka just as shoes and clothing have gradually developed in quality. That helpless item (the burka) came to this land from far-off Arabia—would we ascend the utmost heights of development if we abruptly deported it back?

We have of late become listless, anxious-minded, and fainthearted; this is not because we remain in seclusion—it is a lack of education. How our mental faculties have withered with this absence of enlightenment. The faintheartedness of womankind has gradually been passed on to young boys. When a five-year-old boy sees his mother faint at the sight of an insect, will he not think that a bug really is a terrifying thing?

Here I must add that the blame for passing out at the sight of maggots and insects is not simply our own. The highly civilized ladies of England are not without fault. In the book *Gulliver's Travels* we find an account of Doctor Gulliver's terrified exploration of Brobdingnag's agricultural areas. A Brobdingnagian lifts Gulliver in his hand to show him to his wife! On seeing Doctor Gulliver, the Brobdingnagian woman lets out a fearful scream in exactly the same way an Englishwoman would when petrified by an insect, a maggot, or a spider!! Because the Brobdingnagian giantess thinks the doctor is some kind of tiny worm! So the dread of bugs does not disappear even in those who have abandoned purdah!!

To eliminate the dread of insects we need true enlightenment—through which the brain and mind will be developed (cultured).[11] If we do not receive a higher level of education, society will not develop either. So long as we are not at the same level as men in the intellectual sphere, the hope of development is mere futility. We will have to exercise knowledge in all its forms.

Lacking education, we have become incapable of gaining independence. Because we have become incapable, we have lost independence. To preserve their petty self-interest, blinkered men have forever cheated us of education. Forward-looking brothers are now able to understand that this harms and oppresses them too. They are busying themselves to awaken and uplift. I have said this before: "Men and women are two parts of a single reality. If you abandon one part, the other is incapable of development." I say this again and will repeat it a hundred times if necessary.

I now humbly submit this to my brothers—take the money they lavish to ornament their daughters in jewelry of gold and pearls and try to use it to adorn them with the beauty of knowledge. The satisfaction of reading a single book filled with wisdom is more than a hundred times greater than the pleasure of putting on ten pieces of jewelry. It is thus necessary to let go of body-beautifying decoration and extend women's desires to the benefits of knowledge's beauty. Here is a priceless ornament—

---

11   Translator's note: with the exception of the Bengali copula, the phrase "brain o [and] mind cultured" appears in English within parenthesis in the original.

Thieves cannot take it by plunder,
Kinfolk cannot divide it,
In being given it diminishes not,
So it is said that knowledge is the greatest treasure.

I add a few more lines to this:

Fire cannot burn it,
Waters cannot drown it,
Eternally indestructible, this priceless gem—
This grace remains with you lifelong.

So I say let the money for jewelry be used to set up schools for girls.[12] But I am not confident that my sisters will easily abandon their jewelry for the benefits of school like this. It is sad to say—it seems my sisters have been counted as a species of domestic property! So just as a table is adorned with petals, curtains are adorned with garlands of flowers, beads, or other such things, a woman-householder thinks it essential to adorn her daughter-in-law with heaps of ornaments! Our brothers have still not given up the mockery of sometimes calling us "a kind of rack for storing gold and silver." Then again, "thieves do not listen to moral parables!"

However that may be, purdah is still not a stumbling-block on the path of knowledge. At present we lack women teachers. If we fill this lack and have self-governed schools and colleges, we can obtain the benefits of a higher education and observe the rules of purdah. It is possible that no Muslim will advance into the educational field if we move below the level of purdah needed.[13]

---

12   Translator's note: Rokeya uses the phrase "zenana schools" (in quotation marks) where I have translated "schools for girls." Since the zenana (apartments for women) is not exclusively inhabited by younger women, the phrase can be taken in the broader sense of educational institutions for women of any age.

13   After I had finished writing this essay, part of a speech titled "The Purdah of Ignorance" given by the current Provincial Governor, Sir Andrew Fraser, came to my attention. He said: "Let the efforts of educationists be first directed to the instruction of our girls *within the purdah*, and let woman begin to exercise her chastening influence on society in spite of the system of seclusion, which only time can modify and violent efforts to shake which can only arouse opposition to female education, instead of doing any immediate practical good in the direction

My hope is that now our highly educated sisters will be able to understand that on the whole the burka is not such a bad thing.

---

of emancipation of women" (Quoted in the *Telegraph* newspaper, March 8). Note the surprising resemblance to our own opinions in those of the honorable Provincial Governor.

Translator's addition: the quote from Andrew Fraser is in English in the original.

WOMAN-PRISONER

PREFACE

"Woman-Prisoner" collects a number of tragicomic historical and eyewitness factual events. Brother and sister readers will no doubt laugh at various points, but at several others they will be moved to sympathy; and I believe they will be unable not to shed a few tears at the untimely death of "Tahera."

Mr. Mohammad Khayrul Khan has taken on the entire burden of publishing "Woman-Prisoner" with great enthusiasm. It is due to his zeal that it has appeared in book form. I express my heartfelt thanks for this.

Mr. Abdul Karim, B.A., M.LC., a greatly respected and wise retired School-Inspector, has generously written the introduction to "Woman-Prisoner." For this I express my heartfelt gratitude.

I have gathered beautiful pebbles on my travels in Kurseong and Madhupur; I have gathered multicolored, variously shaped seashells while walking the beaches of Orissa and Madras. And for the past twenty-five years of living to serve society I have gathered curses from rigid phony mullahs.

Saintly Rabi'a of Basra said, "Oh Allah! If I pray for fear of Hell, then fling me to Hell; and if I pray in hope of Paradise, may Paradise be forbidden me." By the grace of Allah, may I now too have courage to speak of my service to society in this way.

Since each and every hair on my body is sinful, I do not beg forgiveness from my brother-and-sister readers for the faults of this book.

Humbly,

—THE AUTHOR

INTRODUCTION

The author of *Woman-Prisoner* has opened up another avenue in our society's mode of thought. Many have gained renown through writing various types of history. But no one has yet written the history of India's oppressed woman prisoners.

Reading the book, one point keeps coming to mind—how did we get to this place! It would probably not be an overstatement to say that Muslim society was once an ideal for the entire world and that now a huge part of this society has become ridiculous to almost the entire world.

There are the female heroes Khawla and Razia on horseback who led male cavalrymen to war, and here are Bengali Muslim women giving everything up to the hands of thieves as they shed silent tears.

I profoundly believe that *Woman-Prisoner* will open people's eyes and minds.

Finally, I thank the writer for her genuine courage. I urge the hearts and eyes of brother- and sister-readers toward *Woman-Prisoner*.

—Abdul Karim (B.A., M.L.C.)

DEDICATION

This volume is vouchsafed
With devotion
To the memory of my deeply honored mother
The late Musammat Rahatunnesa Sabera Chaudhurani

My caring mother was exceedingly favorable toward the seclusion-system. I here recall an incident from my childhood. To make the journey between Calcutta and Rangpur at that time, you had to take a steamer from Sara Ghat to cross the river. We were once going to Calcutta; my little sister was only two years old. She and I were sealed up in a palanquin with mother. This palanquin was put on the steamer deck and we began to cross the river. It was summer. Inside the palanquin that was bound tight with a sheath of thick fabric, my baby sister began to cry: "waah, waah." Mother tried desperately to shut her up. But not one of God's servants sitting beside the palanquin thought it necessary to bring the weeping child outside. I have dedicated this book to her sacred memory as a true sign of devotion.

WOMAN–PRISONER

For a long time now we have become accustomed to living in prison. Thus we—and especially I myself—have nothing to say against prison. If you ask a fishwife, "Is the stench of rotten fish good or bad?" what will she reply?

Here I make a gift of describing some of our personal experiences to our sister-readers—I hope they like it.

At this point it must be said that all over India imprisonment of a family's young women is not simply observed to keep them from men, but also from women. No woman beside the closest relatives and female household servants is permitted to see an unmarried girl.

Married women, too, keep themselves veiled in purdah against female traveling entertainers and performers of various types. She who maintains the best purdah, who best hides in some household corner like an owl, well, she is the noblest of all.

Even urban ladies flee at the sight of English missionary women. And if they catch sight of a sari-clad Christian or Bengali woman—let alone an Englishwoman—they go to their rooms and bolt the door.[1]

[1]

This is a really old story. In a village named Pairaband, deep in Rangpur district, around one or two in the afternoon, the daughters of the zamindar's household were doing their ritual ablutions in preparation for midday prayer.[2] Everyone had finished except "Miss A",

---

1 Translator's note: in a conventional usage, Rokeya writes "Bengali" to signify an Indian Hindu woman.

2 Translator's note: zamindar, a word we will encounter frequently, is an entirely colloquial term for an agrarian landlord. Signifying a social relation of class difference and property rights, it derives from the Persian *zamin* (land, earth) and *-dar* (keeper, holder). While zamindar was lexicalized into Indic languages in

called Sahebzadi, who was still washing in the courtyard. Pitcher in hand, Alta's Ma was pouring water for the daughter's ablution.[3] Right at that moment a very tall and burly Afghan woman arrived in the courtyard.[4] Oh no! What a disaster! The pitcher fell from the hands of Alta's Ma. She began to scream—"Aah, aah! What's this guy doing here!" The woman replied, laughing, "A guy! I'm a guy?" Hearing this much, Sahebzadi "A" ran breathless for dear life to her aunt. Gasping and shaking she said, "Auntie! There's a woman wearing trousers!" The lady of the house asked fretfully, "Did she see you?" "Yes!" replied "A" in tears. The other daughters had broken off their prayers and rushed to bolt all the doors so that the Kabuli woman could not catch sight of these maidens. The way they locked the doors you'd probably think it was for fear of a tiger or a bear.

[2]

This too is a historical incident. A gentleman of Patna invited many ladies to celebrate a wedding at his house. Several arrived at evening-time. Begum Hashmat was among them. A maidservant was opening the door of each palanquin and giving its illustrious female passenger a hand getting down. The bearers take the palanquin away and the next one arrives. Some bearers yelled, "Maid! Passenger coming in." The maid was slow to appear. The bearers set down their "passenger" as they waited for the maid to come to Hashmat Begum's palanquin, taking care to move it aside for the following arrival. Then, when the next palanquin came along, the maid duly opened its door and escorted the wedding guest away.

Wintertime. The empty palanquins had been parked in a group around the base of a banyan tree and their "passengers" disembarked. Nearby, the bearers were cooking a fabulous dinner. They had received

---

the Mughal era, it came to apply to landlords of any religious affiliation (i.e. not just Muslim) and its linguistic form has several regional variants. For example, in Rokeya's usage, a more accurate transliteration from her Bengali would be *jamidar*.
3   Translator's note: "Alta's Ma": the mother of Alta. A conventional way of referring to an adult without having to use their proper name; in this case a servant of the family.
4   Translator's note. The word I have translated as "Afghan woman" is "Kabuli" (with a feminine inflection), literally someone from Kabul, but used more generally in Bengali to refer to traders from Afghanistan who traveled regionally in this era.

splendid ingredients from the marriage house. No more work this night, so they are exuberant—some sing, some smoke tobacco, some eat. The joyous feasting continues past two in the morning.

Meanwhile, the guests sitting to dine in the women's chambers noticed something. Begum Hashmat and her six-month-old baby aren't there. Some said, "Maybe she didn't come because the baby is so small." Some said, "I saw her all decked out to come." And so on.

Next morning the guests were going through their usual departure preparations. One by one the empty palanquins appeared, each to pick up its "passenger." After a while an "empty" palanquin arrived, and on opening its door what should come into view but Begum Hashmat with the infant in her lap! She had spent the long December night sat like this in the palanquin.

The bearers had moved the palanquin away before she had been able to get out—but to ensure they would not hear her voice she hadn't even made a peep. She had also taken utmost care to prevent the baby from crying. If someone heard, they would open the palanquin door and see! What is the glory of the woman-prisoner if not to suffer in silence?

⌊ 3 ⌋

An incident from about forty to forty-five years back. The women of several noble Bengali zamindari families—grannies, aunties, daughters et cetera went on Haj together. There were twenty to twenty-five of them. Once they had arrived at Calcutta train station, their male chaperones had to go elsewhere on business. One trusted male relative was left in charge of these noble begums. He was addressed as Haji Saheb by all respectable folk, and we too will call him that. Haji Saheb did not dare let the noble begums sit in the waiting room. His counsel was for each woman to put on her heaviest burka and squat down on the railway platform. Haji Saheb covered them with a big heavy rug. In that state the poor things looked like a load of luggage or sacks of stuff. For God knows how long, these gentlewomen waited like this—and it is by His infinite mercy that they did not suffocate to death.

At the train's arrival time a railway officer said in broken Hindi to Haji Saheb, "Munshi! Shift yer bags out of here. Train's arriving right

now. Platform's got to be clear except people. No baggage allowed."
Wringing his hands, Haji Saheb said, "Sir, this isn't luggage, it's women."
Giving one of the "sacks" a kick, the railway officer said, "Yeah, yeah,
move all this stuff right now." On account of their purdah, the ladies,
having taken a kicking, didn't make a peep.

[4]

A certain gentleman was employed in the Orissan city of Rajkanika.
His household consisted of his mother, two sisters, and his wife.
Monsoon season. In his lodgings four punkah-pulling coolies took
turns working the fans day and night. The master left for a work tour;
at night a maidservant slept in his wife's room. His female relatives
were in another room.

In that region people don't use a lot of bedlinen in the hot season.
At night, a heavy downpour of rain made the master's wife feel cold,
but she didn't ask the maidservant to call out and stop the fanning. As
the cold gradually became unbearable, she first pulled the bedsheets
over herself. This did not alleviate the cold, so she pulled the rug and
the quilt over herself. But the accursed punkah coolies kept working
the fans harder and harder. So with no other recourse, the young wife
wrapped herself in all the bedding and lay under the bed.

The next morning one of the maids came in to sweep the room and,
seeing some big white thing under the bed, gave it a whack with her
broom. At the blow of the broom, the young wife suddenly rolled aside.
The poor maid was mortified.

[5]

A Bihari gentleman was traveling westward on East India Rail with
his wife. He didn't put his wife in the ladies' compartment but kept
her with him. He bought second-class tickets for them both. Madam
Begum was wearing a burka. At one point, the train stopped at a station while the husband was in the bathroom. Another passenger, not
finding another place to sit, entered the compartment and timorously
sat down, putting his face out of the window. Meanwhile, after coming
out of the bathroom, the aforesaid husband saw that his wife wasn't

there. What to do—it's a moving train! The gentleman traveler got off at the next station. The husband we've mentioned also got down and reported to the station police that his wife had disappeared between this station and the other one.

The unfortunate police telegrammed various stations to look for a woman in a black burka. A constable said, "Let's give this train compartment a quick once-over." The constable noticed a black thing under the husband's seat, and as he heaved it out the husband yelled, "Hey, get off, get off, that's my wife!" It was soon learned that she had hidden herself beneath the seat as soon as she saw the new gentleman traveler.

[6]

In Dhaka district, a zamindar's huge brick mansion caught fire in the middle of the day. Everything was burning to ashes. As well as trying as far as possible to get the belongings out, people also deliberated about the need to rescue the ladies of the house. Sudden need for palanquins. But where to get three or four palanquins, especially in this rustic backwater? It was finally decided that the ladies should make their escape by being put under a large, colorful mosquito-net, held up at each of the outer four corners by a man. This was done. Hounded by fire, the four men supporting the mosquito-net began to run; unable to keep up, the ladies inside tripped over, smashing teeth, breaking noses, tearing clothes. As they fled through the rice fields and thorny bushes, the mosquito-net was also torn to shreds.

What else could they do? The ladies sat in a paddy field. That evening, after the fire had been put out, a palanquin came and took them home one by one.

[7]

About twenty-five years back, a wedding was taking place at a certain Bengali zamindar's house. The house reverberated with guests. The feasting did not break off until two in the morning; now it's time for everyone to sleep. But thieves and burglars won't be asleep—this is their moment to raid.

A thief entered by tunneling a hole in the wall. A watchman heard the burglar's sounds and went to alert the head of the household, actually five or six brothers. Each one armed with a hatchet, they roamed every corner of the house in search of the thief! If they catch the thief they'll chop him to pieces with their hatchets. Ah—the sheer arrogance of this crook!

The ladies saw the thief inside the house and cowered under the bedsheets—in utter silence as if they lacked even the courage to breathe. To the point that the "person unknown" could not pick up the sound of breath. The thief fearlessly cracked the safe and removed all the cash and jewelry. Then, one by one, he took the pieces of jewelry that each lady was wearing. Seeing this, the ladies hastily removed their nose rings, earrings, and necklaces, and laid them on their pillows. This was extremely convenient for the thief—why should he unreasonably touch the noses, ears, and necks of these noble ladies? There was a new bride in the bedchamber. The poor thing took off her nose ring, but her bell-like earrings and various other ornaments got incredibly tangled up with one another—so much so that she couldn't get them off. Mr. Thief waited a while for decency's sake, then took out a penknife, cut off both the bride's ears, packed them in his jewelry-bag, and disappeared through the hole in the wall.

This catastrophe was happening in the house. The men were waiting for the thief outside, hatchets in hand. But the ladies didn't make a peep—so the "person unknown" would not hear the sound of their voices. Only when the thief was safely outside did they begin to scream and wail!

Sister-reader! This is how we maintain the honor of the prison system.

[8]

A house caught fire. The mistress of the house shrewdly and swiftly put all the jewelry into a handbag. As she reached the door, she saw that a group of men was putting out the fire. Rather than coming face-to-face with them outside, she went indoors and sat under the bed with the bag in her hand. That's how she burned to death; but she wasn't outside among men. All praise the prison of respectable family women.

[9]

A respected Islamic scholar died. His only son and wife were left. The scholar had not saved very much, so his family was left in great hardship. With immense difficulty, the widow had some jewelry made for the son's wedding. The jewelry was really expensive. A few days before the wedding, thieves broke through a wall and entered the house. The widow was sleeping inside alone with a single maidservant. Hearing the thieves, she sat up and very quietly roused the maid. The thieves thought—Done for, let's split.

But one of them said, "Hey, let's hold on a minute and see what happens." What happened was pretty funny.

Following her mistress's signal, the servant hung up a piece of cloth in front of the bed to make a screen. Then, showing the thieves a bunch of keys, she said, "Hey guys! Don't come around this side. I'll open the safe and give you anything you want." Next, she removed all the most expensive cloths and ornaments and gave them to the thieves. Fingering and sifting the jewelry to inspect it, they said, "Where's the nose ring? In the safe, right?" At the mistress's sign the servant said, "Mercy! Don't come round this side. Ma'am's only kept the nose ring because the wedding is the day after tomorrow. No more jewelry left. How's there to be a wedding without a nose ring? If you want the nose ring, then take it, go on. Don't come this side of the curtain."

The delighted thieves departed, talking among themselves. It was then three or four in the morning. Drunk on the ecstasy of such an easy triumph, they were talking loudly. The night watchman heard them on the road and went in pursuit. They ran for it. One of the thieves tripped, fell over, and was caught by the watchman. He was forced to take the watchman back to the burgled house. By then it was dawn.

When he arrived, the watchman found that the mistress still had not come out from behind the curtain—"in case those oafs come back." If they caught sight of her! She had also forbidden the servant from calling out in case any men heard the noise and came into the house. She had given up everything to the thieves to preserve the honor of the prison system.

[10]

A zamindar's wife traveled to her younger brother's parents-in-law to collect his wife. One day she appeared and saw the new bride's sister-in-law serving food to the bride. There was a green chili on the plate. She naively asked, "So our wife likes eating fiery food then?" The wife's sister-in-law said, "Oh yes, she eats really fiery stuff!"

Later, she was traveling back to Calcutta by boat. They had to stay several days on the boat. During this time she told the cook to put extra chili in the food. The truth is, the new wife was not at all used to eating peppery food. She had merely been smelling the fragrance of the green chili at mealtime to whet her appetite. So her sister-in-law had jokingly remarked that she loved eating chili. Consequently, the poor thing's life was a misery.

The young wife's new sister-in-law would toss green chili into puffed rice, sit down with her, and lovingly feed her. Tears fell from the young wife's eyes; her mouth and tongue burned; but she would not tell the elder sister-in-law that she couldn't stand chili! Oh calamity! She's a new bride. This is her elder sister-in-law. She wouldn't speak up even to save her life!

[11]

I went to Arrah in 1924. My two granddaughters were getting married on the same day and I had been invited. At home we called the girls Maju and Shabu. The poor things were in prenuptial seclusion chambers. In Calcutta, prospective brides have to serve five or six days jailed in these seclusion chambers before the marriage. But here in Bihar the girls are locked up in solitary confinement for six to seven months until they're half dead.

When I went to Maju's jail-cell I could never stay long—my breath would gag in that confined space. One day I finally opened the window a crack. Within two minutes, along came a female superintendent and said "Chilly air coming in" as she closed the window. I couldn't remain any longer and left. I was unable to stay even a moment in Shabu's jail-cell. But those wretches remained in their cramped cells for six months. This is how we are habituated to imprisonment.

[12]

A Hindu bride from western India went for a ritual dip in the Ganges with her mother-in-law and husband. After bathing, she couldn't find her mother-in-law and husband in the crowd. Finally, she started following a gentleman. A little later the police surrounded them. A constable accosted the gentleman and said, "You're taking off with someone else's wife." The man looked around in surprise: What's this! Some man's wife behind him holding the hem of his loincloth! When the bride was questioned, she replied that she always veiled her head—she'd never properly seen her husband. Her husband wore a yellow-bordered dhoti; this is what she had seen. And noticing this gentleman in a yellow-bordered dhoti she had gone with him.

[13]

Listen to an incident from today (June 28, 1929). The father of a school-girl has written a lengthy letter saying that because the school bus doesn't go down their alley his daughter has to walk home wearing a burka and accompanied by a maidservant.[5] Yesterday a man was passing through the alley with a container of tea. He collided with Hira (the daughter) spilling tea all over her clothes, which were ruined. I gave the letter to one of our teachers and asked her to investigate. What follows is a translation of the report she gave in Urdu:

"During my inquiry I discovered that Hira's burka has no eyeholes. (Hira's burka has no eyes).[6] Other students reported that from the schoolbus they had seen that the maid holds Hira very close as she walks her home. Hira can't walk properly in a burka without eyeholes—once she stumbled over a cat—she often trips up. Yesterday it was Hira who crashed into the tea-carrier and made him drop the tea."[7]

Now see, she's only nine years old—such a young girl has to go out

---

5 Translator's note: Rokeya is describing an incident concerning a student from the school she founded in Kolkata.

6 Translator's note: the parenthesis is an Urdu phrase transliterated into Bengali.

7 I have just come across an article in the monthly journal *Mohammadi*, in which Mrs. Amina Khatun writes: "Going around all the time with nose, face, and eyes covered up (it is possible to bump against unknown men in this kind of purdah)— this purdah is unrelated to Islam."

on the streets in a "blind burka." If she doesn't, the prison's honor will not be sustained!

[14]

An event from about twenty-one or twenty-two years back. A distantly related aunt-in-law of mine was traveling from Bhagalpur to Patna. She had only a single maidservant with her. They had to change trains at Kiul. As she boarded the next train, her huge burka became all tangled up and she got wedged between the train car and the platform edge. There was no other woman at the station at that moment except my aunt's maidservant. When the porters ran forward to help her out, the maidservant forbade it for mercy's sake: "Stay back! No one touches Ma'am's person." Alone, she fiercely yanked and pulled but couldn't get my aunt out. After waiting for about half an hour, the train began to move.

As the train scraped against her, my aunt was ground to bits. Where is her burka—and where is she! A station full of people watched this hair-raising episode in awe. None were permitted to come to her aid. Later, her crushed body was taken to a warehouse. Her maid wept grievously and fanned her with air. After eleven hours in this condition my aunt perished. What an awful death!

[15]

On the occasion of a marriage at the house of a great man of Hooghly, many respectable wives had congregated in a room. Around midnight, they had the feeling someone was shoving the door from outside. Now forcefully, now softly, pushing the door in various ways. The ladies all arose, trembling intensely—a thief must be breaking down the door to get into the house. And he'll catch sight of the ladies! Then, a crafty and domineering lady put on most of her jewelry, packed away the rest and hid it. She donned her burka and opened the door. Outside was...a she-dog! Her two pups happened to be inside the room, and she was outside. She had been pushing at the door to get to her pups.

[16]

A wealthy man of the Bihari gentry was traveling to Darjeeling. He had a dozen pieces of "human luggage" with him.[8] That is, maternal and paternal aunts et cetera numbering seven women; and five girls aged from six to thirteen years old. Each time they changed train or steamboat they had arranged for palanquins. The palanquins were there at Monihari Ghat, Sakrigali Ghat, and so on. The women were packed into the palanquins right on the steamboat decks. Then, when it was time to board the train, they were loaded into the baggage car with the palanquins. But along the East Bengal Rail Line there were no more palanquins to be had. They were then obliged to sit in a reserved second-class train car.

At Siliguri station they couldn't get palanquin bearers either. What a gigantic mess—how are these ladies to board the Darjeeling train? Eventually, four men held up two sheets by the corners and the ladies proceeded within the cover of these screens. The accursed sheet-carrying minions were unable to keep in step with each other on the steep and bumpy road. Now the right-hand screen moves ahead and the left-hand screen falls behind; next the left-hand screen advances and the right-hand one moves backward. The poor ladies walked ever-more unsurely—sometimes overtaking the screen and sometimes lagging behind it! Their shoes fell off, their scarves blew away.

[17]

About fourteen years ago there was a teacher from Lucknow at our school—Akhtar Jahan is her name. She also had three daughters in the school. One day, while discussing the topic of modern girls' shamelessness, she expressed unhappiness on the subject of her own daughters' insolence. In the course of the discussion, she told a story about her own days as a new bride: "She was married at eleven years old. At her in-laws' home she had to live in a solitary chamber. A younger sister-in-law came to escort her to the bathroom three or four times a day as needed. One day for some reason she heard nothing from this girl for a long time. In the meantime, the poor young wife felt the call of

---

8 Translator's note: "human luggage" appears in English type in parentheses after Rokeya's "manab bojha."

nature and got agitated. In Lucknow, girls are given the dowry gift of a large copper paan chest. Her own capacious paan chest was in the chamber. She opened the chest, took out the box of betel nuts and poured the nuts into a handkerchief. The thing she filled that box with, which she then hid under the bed, well it doesn't bear writing about. When the maid from her paternal home arrived to make the bed in the evening, the weeping girl clung to her and relayed the terrible state of the box. The maid comforted her, saying, 'It's alright, don't cry. I'll get the box re-plated tomorrow and bring it back.[9] Keep the betel nuts in the handkerchief for now.'"

[18]

A certain doctor of Lahore reports his similar experiences visiting female patients thus:

Normally when a doctor visits, two maidservants stand at the head and foot of the patient's bedstead holding a thick blanket over her. The doctor puts his hand through a hole in the blanket to take the patient's pulse.[10]

A respectable lady was sick with pneumonia. I said her lungs must be examined. I'll make the examination from the back. The command was this: "The maid will place the stethoscope tube wherever you say!" Everyone knows that a diagnosis can be made only by examining the lungs from various points. But I had no choice other than to follow the master's order. The maidservant put the tube under the blanket a little over the midriff area (above the leggings). After a while I was amazed to find I couldn't hear a thing. Why? With great audacity I lifted the blanket slightly and took a look—only to see that the tube was resting on her waist. I got up and left in annoyance.[11]

---

9   Translator's note: "tinning" appears in English type in parentheses, referring to the tin plating that will restore the inside of the feces-soiled box.

10   A non-purdah woman once asked me: (if there were no lady-doctor available and it was a man) how would you let the doctor examine your tongue? Wouldn't you have to make a hole in the blanket and put your tongue through so he could see? I entreat my sister-readers to answer this question and the following one of my own. If you had to show your eyes, teeth, or ears to a doctor, how would you do it?

11   Listen to the respected doctor's own words—"What in the world! And the nawab asked, what have you found out? What the hell could I tell him about what

[19]

This is the summary of a certain railway passenger's report: I bought tickets at the station and did some mental arithmetic. With three Inter-Class tickets we were entitled to bring two and a half maunds' weight of luggage, but our things didn't weigh less than five maunds.[12] After much thought I decided not to check it all in. Who would come to inspect if I put them into the women's carriage instead?

*   *   *

My son asked—Got any living luggage with you?
   Don't I just! A perfect pair! One old crone, the other dry as a bone.
The boy said—There you go, then!

*   *   *

When I awoke it was quite late at night.
   I figured the train had stopped at a large station. I suddenly realized it was probably Baharampur station. Right when I opened the door to disembark I thought I could hear somebody yelling my name—"Tunu, O Tunu, we've got into a terrible mess. Help, Tunu!"
   It was a feminine voice, pitiful too. I hurriedly climbed down. I saw the two old women standing there weeping profusely. All the luggage had been pulled off. Several porters were standing around them.
   I was enraged. It was disgraceful that the T.T.C., that is, the train ticket collectors, should inspect the women's car at night and unload all the luggage. I yelled at the porters and told them to put our things back on the train. I harshly berated the porters again and told them I was going to file a report against the T.T.C.
   Grandma wept and said, "But Tunu, we've arrived."
   Finally, a porter summoned the courage to speak. "Sir, you're here."
   I said to grandma, "So the T.T.C. didn't check and throw you out— we arrived and you got off. You could have told me earlier. What are you crying for?"

I'd found out?"
12 Translator's note: a maund is an Indian unit of weight. One maund equals approximately 82 pounds or 37 kilos. Five maunds is thus about 410 pounds.

[20]

A certain respectable lady of Punjab wrote the story printed below in an Urdu newspaper:

We lived in a village for a while. A member of the local gentry invited us to his house. I was deeply shocked by the excessive tyranny to which the young girls of the family were subjected.

When we arrived I asked, Where are the daughters of the house? I was informed that they were in the kitchen. I wanted to meet them in person, and I was asked to go in there alone. The kitchen was horribly hot and incredibly small. But seeing no other option, I sat down and began to talk with these downtrodden but sweet-spoken girls.

Taking pity, a merciful woman said to us, "Go up to the roof; careful, and don't let anyone see."

I figured perhaps there might be a dread of encountering men, so that's why she said to go carefully and covertly. But I later learned that the purdah was observed against regular female visitors. Following the aforementioned lady's order, two women held up a thick purdah-sheet, and we went upstairs inside its screen.

Once upstairs there were more problems. I had supposed that there would be a comfortable room to sit in. But there was nothing up there. First, burning sun; second, nowhere to sit. Half-dried dungcakes strewn across the rooftop; their stink made me sick to my stomach. A maidservant effortlessly dragged out a couch, and there we all sat. Music was playing downstairs; the party was in full swing. But these wretched unmarried girls, judged as sinners, sat in the sun gagging on the stench of dungcakes. No one considered their comfort in the slightest.

[21]

There was dancing and singing to celebrate an auspicious festival-day at a Bengali zamindar's house. The enormous marquee under which the dancers were performing could be seen from the entry-room of the house. But none of the ladies of the house ever visited that entry-room. The ladies did not have the good fortune to enjoy dance and musical performance.

The zamindar had a three-year-old daughter. The girl was

wonderfully fair-complexioned. She was lovingly called sugar-doll by some and milky-doll by others. Her name was Sabera. That morning, the instrumental prelude to Raag Bhairavi awoke the birds and they began to chirp. Sabera's "playmate" (a modern word for "nursemaid") woke up. She fancied going to see a bit of dancing. But Sabera was still sleeping. So the playmate picked up the sleeping child and went to the entry-room to watch the dancing.

When there's something that you fear, its danger's yet more near.[13] Just then, the master was coming from the outer to the inner chambers. He saw the playmate, with Sabera in her arms, lifting the blind slats and watching the spectacle. He had a thick bamboo staff in his hand and began giving the playmate a severe beating with it. The ladies came to the entry-room when they heard the playmate's screams. A blow landed on Sabera's thigh. A friend of the zamindar's brother came forward and said, "What are you doing, young brother! What are you doing! You'll beat your daughter?" The rain of blows stopped instantly. The zamindar angrily spoke: "I don't care if this bitch sees the dancing herself, but why'd she bring my daughter to look?"

But actually the child was fast asleep with her head resting on the playmate's shoulder—the little one hadn't seen a thing. The whole house was in uproar—the master himself was utterly mortified at the ugly black bruise made by the stick's pounding on her milky thigh. We are kept prisoners in jail through such beatings with sticks.

[22]

One evening a gentleman was pacing the busy platform of Sealdah Station as he waited for a train. Another gentleman was standing nearby. A heap of bedding and so forth was beside him. Feeling a little tired, the first gentleman went and sat on this heap of bedding. As soon as he sat down the luggage began to wriggle—he immediately leaped up in fright. The standing gentleman ran over and said angrily, "Sir, what are you doing? Why'd you go and sit on the women?" Completely

---

13   Translator's note: this translates Rokeya's use of the rhyming Bengali proverb, "jekhane bagher bhoy, sekhanei rat hoy." Literally: You fear tigers just as night is falling. This expresses the idea of a threat arriving as it is anticipated, or a danger arriving unexpectedly soon.

flabbergasted, the poor man said, "Forgive me, Sir! I don't see so well in the evening gloom. I thought this was a pile of bedding and sat down. I was scared witless when it started to move!"

[23]

Let's put others' stories aside. I'm going to tell one of my own about this. As soon as I was five years old I had to enter purdah, even in front of women. I understood absolutely nothing of why I couldn't appear before other people; yet I had to observe purdah. Men were of course prohibited from entering the women's quarters; I hadn't encountered their oppression. But women had unrestricted access—and still I had to remain hidden from their gaze. Women from the neighborhood would suddenly drop in; someone would give me a meaningful glance and I'd flee anywhere for dear life—sometimes for the cover of the kitchen's wicker door, sometimes into a straw mat that had been rolled up by one of the maidservants, sometimes for shelter under a bed.

When hens see a bird of prey in the sky they make a signal and their chicks rush to hide beneath mother's wings. That's exactly how I had to flee. But chicks have a constant natural refuge at their mother's breast to which they can always go. There was no such reliable, unthreatened place for me. And chicks naturally understand their mother's signs—I had no such innate instinct.[14] Consequently, if I ever failed to understand the meaningful glance, not disappear, and run into someone by accident, the considerate mistresses of the house would rarely hold back from saying things about "how shameless, how corrupted, are the young women of this accursed epoch."

When I was five years old and living in Calcutta at the home of my second sister-in-law's aunt, two maidservants came from Bihar to see her. They had a "free passport" and would roam all around the house, and I, like a faun fleeing in deadly fear, would scurry all over the place—behind a door or under a table. On the third floor was an abandoned garret room. My nursemaid would carry me up and deposit me there early in the morning. I'd spend almost the entire day there, famished. Once the pair of Bihari maidservants had made

---

14 Translator's note: Rokeya uses the word "dharma" here followed by "instinct" in English type in parentheses: "I had no such innate [svabhabik] dharma (instinct)."

a thoroughgoing inspection of the entire house, they discovered the garret. A nephew of my own age, Halu, came running to warn me of this disaster. What luck, there was a wooden four-poster bed there and I got under it and stayed there, holding my breath. The terror—in case these heartless women hear my breathing and take a peek under the bed! There were all sorts of beaten-up boxes, woven stools, and so on in there. Poor Halu, using his feeble strength (he was six), dragged all that stuff over and surrounded me with it. No one came regularly to see if I had food. Occasionally, Halu would show up in the garret when he was playing around the house and I would tell him I was hungry and thirsty. Sometimes he would bring me a glass of water, sometimes a bit of crisped rice. Sometimes he'd go off to bring food and not come back—a little kid, they forget things. I was in that state for around four days.

[24]

In the district of Bihar, the womenfolk of noble households do not ordinarily board the train when traveling by rail. They are thrust into a palanquin covered with finespun wool which is loaded onto the train's freight wagon. The result is that the ladies cannot see the slightest part of the journey. They traverse the land like Brooke Bond tea packed in a vacuum tin. But an aristocratic family of Calcutta has trumped even this. If the ladies of the house set out for anywhere by train, each of them is first sealed into a palanquin with a couch, a palm-leaf fan, a pitcher of water, and a glass. With father or son observing, the servants would next perform the following steps on each palanquin: (1) pack it in a cover of finespun wool; (2) sew a layer of waxed cloth over this; (3) sew an enclosure of tough red twill over that; (4) next, stitch some sheets of Bombay cloth on top; (5) finally, after all this, sew on a wrapping of sackcloth. This stitching business goes on for three or four hours—and the master of the house stands there the entire time keeping strict watch. The bearers are then summoned and the palanquins are loaded into the train's brake van. Then, once the destination has been reached, more men undo the successive layers of stitching under the eye of a supervisor. The servants depart once the stitching is off and only the woolen covering remains. Next, the lord himself, with his close relatives and womenfolk, open the palanquin door and release the half-dead, unconscious prisoners. They normally apply rose-water and fan the women's heads, spoon water into their mouths, sprinkle water on their eyes and faces, and keep the fresh air coming. The ladies recover after a couple of hours of nursing.

[25]

In section eleven of "Woman-Prisoner" I wrote that in 1924 I went to Arrah to attend the wedding of my two granddaughters. But I saw nothing of Arrah town beside that house and the sky. I talked with my "daughter" about this (actually, she's the second wife of my son-in-law after my daughter died).[15] She implored me: "Mother, if in all your benevolence you wish to see the town, please bless these lowly ones and take us along. We've been here seven years but never seen a bit of town." The newlywed Maju and Shabu pleaded, "Yes, grandma, you have to ask papa." A few days later I got around to asking my son-in-law to hire a carriage; each day he would very politely inform me that no carriages were available. On the afternoon of my final day, his eleven-year-old son informed us that although a carriage had been hired one of its window blinds was broken. Maju piped up excitedly, "We'll put up a curtain there, for Allah's sake don't send the carriage away." Shabu whispered, "Nice, we'll get a good view from that damaged window." Every time we were ready to board the hired carriage this is what we heard: Please have patience, there's no curtain in there yet.

A while later we went out to the carriage, Praise Allah! We saw that the carriage had been completely covered over with several lengths of Bombay cloth. My son-in-law himself opened the carriage door; once we had boarded he used the cloth to tie it shut. Once the carriage had traveled a little way Maju spoke to Shabu, "Now look through the broken window!" There was a small tear in the curtain. Shabu, Maju and their mother leaned over to see. I did not fight with them to peer through that hole.

15   Translator's note: this may seem confusing to readers aware that the two daughters of Rokeya's body died in infancy. Rokeya's husband had a daughter by his first marriage, and Rokeya relates to her, too, as a daughter and to her husband as a son-in-law. After the death of this daughter, the son-in-law remarried, and the new wife is Rokeya's new "daughter" and the mother of Maju and Shabu.

[26]

In principle, even our names observe purdah. Young women's names are only revealed at marriage when written in the contract. The three daughters of a great zamindar were being married on the same day. The girls' family nicknames were Big Gendla, Middle Gendla, and Little Gendla—no one knew their proper names. An uncle of one of their relatives was the marriage cleric. There were three grooms ranged according to the different ages of the girls. The three grooms were absent from the wedding gathering. For the convenience of our readers, we'll call them No. 1, No. 2, and No. 3.

The cleric was handed a list with the names of the three grooms and three girls. When he started reading the marriage rites he mistakenly got the names of the grooms and girls mixed up and married groom No. 1 to Little Gendla. He wed groom No. 3 to Middle Gendla. Then it was time for Big Gendla to be married to groom No. 2. Middle and Little Gendla were really young, eleven and seven years old, so they didn't speak up. But Big Gendla was nineteen years old. She had secretly listened in on her elders and knew she was being married to groom No. 1. She even knew the groom's name. Consequently, when the cleric brought up the name of groom No. 2 and asked for Big Gendla's "I do," she kept her mouth completely shut. She endured the threats of her mother and aunts and didn't say a thing, at which point her mother lost all patience and said to the cleric, "Yes, Gendla said 'uh-huh.' The marriage is done, how long can this take." He said, "We haven't heard 'uh-huh' from Gendla's mouth, maybe you want me to hitch you with this 'uh-huh'?" The mother punched the girl hard in the back. We didn't ultimately find out whether poor Gendla said 'uh-huh' or not.

When the thirty-year-old groom No. 1 learned via telegram that his marriage had taken place and that he was wedded to the very youngest seven-year-old Little Gendla (instead of nineteen-year-old Big Gendla), he became inflamed with rage. He wrote to his mother-in-law to exchange the girl or else he would sue her for fraud. And so on and so forth.

[27]

An incident from around ten or eleven years back. I have mentioned that in the Bihar area girls are locked up in the "maiden's compartment" for three months before marrying. And sometimes—if there's a domestic incident that delays the wedding—the term of imprisonment in this jailhouse can be up to a year. One miserable girl was a prisoner like this for six months. Her regular arrangements for washing, food and so on were completely neglected. Firstly, Biharis don't particularly like to bathe; and besides, who would go regularly to bathe a girl-prisoner in the "maiden's compartment"? During this time, girls are not permitted to place their feet on the ground—when required, they have to be carried to the bathroom. All movement is strictly forbidden. She must sit all day on a wooden bed hanging her head, and at night there she must lie. She lifts her head to be fed scraps of food by others; others pour water into her mouth from a cup. Tangled hair—so what? She may not brush it herself. In sum, she is dependent on others for absolutely everything. In any case, when after six months this girl was married off, it was discovered that as a result of keeping her eyes closed the whole time she had permanently destroyed her sight.

[28]

An incident from years back. As a result of her immense virtue, an eminent Arab woman visited Calcutta. She had learned to speak some broken Urdu. When hordes of ladies came by palanquin to pay their respects, she got irritated by the sight of the palanquins. Why are they "punished" like this?

One day, a lady from East Bengal arrived. By way of welcome, the Arab woman asked after the health of the visitor's husband, and the Bengali lady pulled her sari hood over her head, replying, "He's a'right. What could happen to em? He's a'right." The poor Arab lady couldn't understand at all why you'd have to pull up your hood when speaking of your husband's condition.

The Arab lady would stop and observe the business of Bengali women and their palanquins with curiosity. One day, a woman in a burka was aboard a palanquin with a two-year-old child on her lap, a paan case, a large wooden box, a bundle of clothing, and a pitcher of water. The woven cane base of the palanquin was damaged, but no one had noticed it beforehand. When the bearers lifted the palanquin, its cane seat began to collapse with a tremendous crack. An armed footman was walking on either side of the palanquin. Addressing the child, they asked, "Young sir what's that cracking sound?" But no reply came from the palanquin. Shortly afterward when they had passed through the gate, the bearers stopped moving as the palanquin felt unusually light. Meanwhile, the burka-wearing lady had fallen through the palanquin's splintered base and was sitting on the ground clutching her son. The bundle of clothing, the paan case, everything was scattered around. She was soaked with water from the smashed pitcher. And yet she didn't even say, "Palanquin, stop!" This kind of mess, and on the streets of Calcutta! The poor Arab woman quickly sent out her maidservant to fetch the lady, saying, "Madam, I really wasn't prepared to witness such a crazy scene."

[29]

I once went to Aligarh for a Ladies' Conference. I saw many kinds of burkas worn by the women attending. One of them had a rather unusual looking burka. Once we'd been introduced, I admired her burka and she said, "Oh, don't—this burka has humiliated me so many times!" Here are all the humiliations that she told me about:

She was an invited wedding guest at a Bengali gentleman's home. As soon as they saw her (the burka-wearer), the children screamed in fright and ran off who knows where. Her husband was acquainted with several other Bengali gentry, so she had to visit all their homes too. But every time she went to one of these houses, the children would scream and kick up a fuss. They would tremble in fear.

Once she came to Calcutta. If she and her burka-wearing friends went out in an open-top automobile, passing boys would say, "Bloody hell! What on earth are those things?" They would say to each other, "Keep quiet! Those ghosts are bound to come out at night." If they saw the women's face-covering niqabs flutter in the breeze they'd say, "Look out, look out! The ghosts are waving their elephant trunks! Run for your life!"

One time she went to Darjeeling. At Ghum station she saw that a crowd had gathered to gawk at a midget. He was about the height of a six- or seven-year-old boy, but his face was that of a man with full beard and mustache. Suddenly she noticed that the crowd had turned its gaze on her with intense curiosity. The onlookers had lost interest in the midget and were staring at this woman in a burka!

Once they had arrived in Darjeeling, they went out for an after-dinner expedition by rickshaw. They saw a huge crowd on The Mall. The army had returned from Tibet that day, and the crowd was there for the sight. The coolie parked the rickshaw on one side of the street and went off to see the spectacle himself. Shortly afterward she noticed that all the spectators were coming by one by one to take a peek at her inside the rickshaw.

If she went out on foot, street-dogs would bark and attack her. Unharnessed mountain ponies started rearing in fright at the sight of her. When visiting a tea garden she noticed that a three- or four-year old girl had picked up a large rock to hit her with.[16]

She was on an outing with a small group of other ladies she knew. They snagged their burkas beside a small stream and all fell into the pebble-strewn mud. Some coolies rushed from the nearby tea garden and helped them up. In a tone of affectionate rebuke they said, "You're wearing shoes and all those veils on top—how're you not going to trip up in that state?" Alas! The ladies' embroidered scarves were spattered with mud; their burkas were soaked through.

Not only that, people in the streets would try to silence their bawling infants by pointing at them and saying, "Shut up, y'see Mecca and Medina going by—there! Evil hags in veils—that's Mecca and Medina!"

[30]

A zamindar had arranged to wed his marriageable daughter to a well-born, wealthy, and highly eligible groom. For some reason, the father of the groom and the father of the girl got into an argument and the marriage was canceled. The bride had never been so upset.

Unable quickly to find another groom, the girl's father arranged a marriage to a dissolute nephew. The poor girl was well acquainted with her cousin's awful habits—often had she prepared hangover cures for the drunkard and tried to clear his head by dousing it with water.

---

16   Note here the difference between Bengalis and Gurkhas. While Bengali children scream and flee in terror, the little Gurkha picks up a rock in self-defense and prepares to attack the object of fear.

So she had a serious objection to this match.

But the bride is mute—she has no power of speech. Her only option is silent weeping. So she wept ceaseless tears from her eyes and gave up eating and drinking. But her cruel parents didn't blink an eye—they would wed her to this drunkard no matter what. In this way our class of phony mullah overlords maintains Islam and the Sharia by wringing its neck.

At the wedding ceremony the bride did not say "I do." Her mother, aunts, etc. begged, pleaded, gently rebuked—to which she responded with floods of tears. Finally, one of them gave the girl a sudden sharp pinch; there was an abrupt "uh-huh!" at the shock. A plaintive sound. With the utterance of this "uh-huh" or "uh" the wedding rite was finalized. Glory to God! All hail prison!

[31]

Once a thief entered the women's compartment at some point on a moving train. The thief nonchalantly began to remove each woman's jewelry in turn. Yet cowering in shame, these timid, powerless, simple, sheltered women put up no resistance. They all just pulled up their veils. "Alas! Alack! What's this man doing here!" Some of them covered up with their niqabs. Later, Mister Thief pulled the train's alarm chain and disembarked safely when it stopped.

[32]

The family nickname for the zamindar of Bhangni is—let's suppose—Baccha Mia.[17] His wife's name is Hasina Khatun. Hasina's father has immense wealth—pots of money. One day Baccha Mia said to his wife, "I need money. Write to your father today and ask for money." Instead of money, a prompt letter of reply arrived explaining the correctness of frugal economics.

Baccha Mia's father-in-law had often given money to his son-in-law. Giving money had now become distasteful. So instead of sending money to his daughter he sent advice. Baccha Mia was enraged by this and prohibited visits to his wife's father's home.

17   Translator's note: literally this means "Mister Baby" or "Mister Child."

There was weeping on the part of the parents; there was silent grief on Hasina's part. They could see each other no more. Some time later, Hasina's brother came to see her.

He did not go directly to Bhangni. He remained a few miles away at his aunt's house in a village called Phulchowki. The morning after he arrived he sent word to Bhangni that he would arrive in the afternoon. Baccha Mia devised a scheme whereby the brother and sister would not be able to meet. He told his wife that someone had been sent from Phulchowki to bring them there. Hasina was aware of her husband's trickery; immediately she did not trust what he said. In some way she was able to know that her brother was coming that afternoon.

Baccha Mia repeated, "Your brother has a headache and won't be able to come today. So aunt has sent Iyar Mahmud Sardar to bring us there. If you don't believe me, come to the entryway and hear it from Sardar himself."

Accordingly, Iyar Mahmud was summoned from outside the entryway door. Once inside, Baccha Mia asked, "Iyar Mahmud! Haven't you just come from Phulchowki?" He replied, "Yes, sir! I come with news—." Baccha Mia swiftly changed the subject and didn't let him go on.

Happy Hasina got ready to go to her aunt's house. A cloth-swathed palanquin was set up for this, and for her maids there were eight smaller litters wrapped in red linen. Baccha Mia's meyana (a type of open palanquin) was prepared. Orderlies, armed footmen, mace-bearers and all the rest set off at one o'clock in the afternoon.

Along the way, as soon as Hasina realized that her palanquin had been mounted upon two dinghies roped together to cross a river, she began to wail. There's no need to cross any river to get to Phulchowki—Allah, oh Allah! What place is her master taking her! And what could a woman prisoner do but weep and strike her head on the palanquin walls?

[33]

About eighteen years ago in Calcutta, a one-and-a-half-year-old infant had come down with fever. The household practiced a particularly severe form of imprisonment—so even though the girl was very little, no he-doctor was allowed to see her. Therefore, a she-doctor was brought in. The household was full of women who had no other qualities beyond a noble benevolence. They crowd around the lady doctor, Miss Gupta. Miss Gupta made the examination and asked that the sick child be bathed in warm water.

Miss Gupta wants warm water—the ladies gape at each other! She wants cold water—they exclaim, "Oh, what! The child's fever will worsen if she's bathed in cold water!" In other words, that day Miss Gupta was unable to make them understand her instructions in the slightest. On the way out, she explained everything to the lord's house-manager and told him she would not come back to this place. With many solicitous pleas and a sixteen-rupee fee, the house-manager persuaded her to come back the next day.

The following day, the ladies of the house again created utter chaos for Miss Gupta, the she-doctor. Seeing the trouble, the house-manager fetched a woman he knew and sent her in to Miss Gupta. When Binapani (the Bengali woman summoned by the house-manager) arrived, she found the lady doctor in a terrible rage. The mistresses of the house were huddled together trembling in fear. Their faces were burning.[18] Finally Miss Gupta roared, "I didn't come here for this madness!"

Binapani quietly asked the ladies of the house what the matter was. They said, we don't understand. She asks for a towel, she asks for a tub, but whatever we give she rubbishes it.

Next she asked Miss Gupta about the reason for her anger. Miss Gupta pointed at her wristwatch and said, "Look at this! I've been here half an hour already and still I haven't got a thing to bathe the baby with." Bina asked warily, "So you don't like the things they are giving you?"

Miss Gupta said, tell me how I'm supposed to like them? I need a bathtub that I can bathe a child in. They give me this measly pint-size cooking pan—so I chuck it out! Tell me, can I put a child in a pan that small? I need a soft, worn-in cloth to wipe the baby with; they give me a new, scratchy towel—so I chuck it out! They proudly show me that

---

18 Translator's note: the last phrase translates the Bengali proverb used by Rokeya: mukhe dhan dile khoi phote. "If you put rice on their faces it would pop into crisps." Khoi is a form of popped rice that is made putting rice grains onto a very hot surface.

they have brand-new towels! They're so holier-than-thou—they think everybody should worship them![19]

Bina finally arranged the right things and helped Miss Gupta bathe the infant. Rage subsided and she began to smile. The ladies of the house breathed a sigh of relief.

[34]

I heard this about the customs of a noble family of Bengal's gentry, that during the wedding ceremony the girls do not verbally consent. Why should some unrelated man hear this little "yes" in her own voice? Consequently, at the wedding service the bride's attorney, the witnesses, her relatives, and the groom's family are on one side of a thick curtain. On the other side the bride sits with the women. There is a bronze platter below the curtain—half of it is on one side, half of it on the other.

Once the wedding formulas have been spoken, a female companion or maid helps the bride make a clang on the platter with a betel-nut cutter. Once the cutter's sound has traveled to the men's side, the marriage ritual is complete.

I remember something else about this. I know a respectable lady from Lucknow. I was paying a visit to her house. When her seven-year-old son was misbehaving she went to hit him and called him a bastard. After he had run off, I asked her frankly whom she was cursing like that—her son or herself? At that, she laughed and replied that when she got married no one asked her agreement even though she was of age. At the marriage party she didn't say a single "yes," "I do." Her marriage was fixed by force. Therefore, her "children are all bastards."

[35]

This is a translation of part of the late Maulvi Nazir Ahmed Khan Bahadur's renowned book describing the sufferings of imprisoned women during the Delhi uprisings:[20]

---

19 Translator's note: the phrase "everybody should worship them!" is in English type in the original.

20 Translator's note: the reference is to Nazir Ahmed, author of *Mirat al Urus*

At ten in the evening an envoy from the British Captain informed my elder brother that they would mount an attack on the rebels at two in the morning. Their cannon were deployed near our house. Consequently, we must flee for our lives before the attack. Our blood ran cold at the very news. But we had no choice.

We were finally obliged to travel on foot. If I think back to that tragic day I still feel both sad and happy. A mistress of the house left behind all her valuables but took her paan chest. The poor women were totally unaccustomed to walking—and now when they had to walk for their lives their shoes were falling off, the waistbands of their pants were getting tangled up in their legs. The wider the flares in their pants, the more extreme difficulty they had in walking. Bitterly annoyed, my elder brother said to them, "You wretched idiots, go make yourselves some bigger muslin pants. Why not add some gold edging to lengthen your waistbands of Lahore silk!"

The poor things were on the market road. They were saved by the providence of nightfall! Which is to say that there were no crowds to witness our current miserable state. Dear me! Everyone's feet were heavy and swollen—they'd take a couple of steps, stumble, fall down, over and over. One of them flopped down in the street; she could walk no further. It wasn't just feet that ached, our entire bodies were in torment. The poor ladies' disgrace was without end.

A little further on we saw thousands of English and Sikh soldiers marching in ranks. We were frightened to death at the very sight of them! So petrified we could not move.

When we had eventually managed to go a bit further, my brother got hold of four donkeys. In the end, the ladies were saved by riding them.

[36]

Wintertime. January cold. From somewhere or other, a man came to the village with his dancing bear. If a novelty arrived in the village it

(The Bride's Mirror), the most widely read Urdu novel of the nineteenth century. It is also generally recognized as the first Urdu novel. The uprising alludes to the 1857 "Mutiny" that began among Indian soldiers recruited to protect and fight for the British. The passages Rokeya translates are from Nazir Ahmed's second novel, *Binat-un-Nash* (Daughters of the Bier, 1872).

had first of all to put in an appearance at the zamindar's house. The bear-trainer accordingly became a guest at this zamindar's house. The bear dance was performed daily in a field to the north of the sprawling mansion—the entire village gathered to see! But the women of the zamindar's house were prohibited from watching the dance.

The young boys and ancient maidservants would return and tell the ladies of the house all about it—the bear dances the khemta dance; the bear dances the thamka dance. How the bear grapples with the bear-trainer; how it uses wrestling holds. And so on. On hearing all these stories, two of the lord's younger daughters-in-law really wanted to see some of this dancing. They did not have to go far: there is a north-facing window in the junior wife's chambers where the slats of the blind just need to be prized open a little to get a clear view.

As soon as they had lifted this wife's blind slats, their four-year-old sister-in-law Zohra ran in saying she wanted to see too. One of them lifted her on her hip to see. Zohra had never been down to the mansion's courtyard. She had never even seen a dog or a cat—and now all at once she saw a bear! The bear was in a wrestling match, and Zohra screamed in fear and fainted at the sight! Forget the bear dance in the field—now they had to deal with Zohra.

Zohra regained consciousness of course, but her fear did not dissipate. At night she suddenly awoke screaming and quaking in terror. Since the condition was evidently urgent, a very expensive doctor was summoned from the far-off district center. The doctor inquired into the whole matter; has the child had some kind of a fright? The thing remained no secret; it came out that she had been terrified by seeing the bear dance.

So the lord began an investigation: who let her see the bear dance? From the nursemaid to the maidservants, everyone unanimously swore that they had not shown the young heiress the bear dance. It finally came out that it was the daughters-in-law. His fury then became extreme. If Zohra dies then she dies; the lord has no problem with that. But according to the laws of this kingdom, how is he supposed to bear the disgrace of having his daughters-in-law gawping at the escapades of unknown men? Shame! Shame! Even the Civil Surgeon, a doctor of another faith, had smirked on hearing that these young women had gone to see the bear dance.

Beside himself with misery and rage, the lord issued a summons to the daughters-in-law. With veils drawn over their faces, the two young women appeared before their father-in-law and, shaking with shame and disgrace (it was wintry-cold, too), sweating, and falling to the ground at his feet, they said:

O Mother Earth! Open up in haste—

Swallow us in You!

And really, what reason is there for purdah-wearers to be on the face of this earth? Gnashing his teeth the lord says, "Listen, daughters—" and becomes speechless with rage. "Hands tremble in fury, eyes turn red"—he could not decide whether to chew on these unseasoned daughters or devour them whole!

[37]

One time, when a train was coming toward Howrah from the west, three burka-clad persons got into the women's car at Bali station. There were many Muslim women in the car. Once the train left, the women noticed with surprise that the new arrivals did not raise the niqabs (face-coverings) on their burkas. They had a feeling that they didn't know what these people intended. And the new passengers were also very tall. The women sought God's blessing, and when the train stopped at Lilua station and the female ticket-collector entered the compartment, they all spoke to her about these burka-wearers. As soon as the ticket-collector turned her attention to them, one of the three leaped out of the train window on the opposite side of the station and fled. Yelling "Police! Police!" the conductress grabbed another of them and raised the niqab. Look—a beard on the face—a mustache! Completely unraveled, she said, "How incredible! Facial hair in a burka!"

[38]

A certain she-doctor of my acquaintance, Miss Saratkumari Mitra, once said, "Well! The hassle if I go to one of your lot's homes—Muslims, I mean! Can't get a bit of warm water in good time, can't even get a piece of rag!"

Once someone was sent from far away to summon her, informing her that the youngest wife of the house had toothache. She went, taking with her whatever dental medication she had as well as thinking to bring the instruments needed to extract teeth if necessary. When she arrived she found that the pain was not dental—it was the pain of childbirth! What does she do now? Jamgaon is eight or nine miles from Bhagalpur town. Impossible to go back so far on that horsedrawn wagon; the horses are worn out. Jamgaon is an outskirt, a village-like place where you would not find a carriage or palanquin.

She somehow got back to Bhagalpur, and as she was returning to Jamgaon with the instruments appropriate for this eventuality the patient entered the critical stage of her labor. Miss Mitra asked the mistress of the house why she had been uselessly summoned with such an untruthful story. In reply, the mistress said, "We used a male servant to call the doctor, so if we hadn't said toothache what could we have said? For shame! How can one speak of the other thing to a man? What kind of woman-doctor are you that you can't understand what people are saying?"

[39]

Our society does not limit itself to just keeping woman prisoners shut away. Was not Hazrat Ayesha Siddiqa ready to be married at nine years old. This is why the daughters of respectable Muslim homes are prohibited from laughing loudly, speaking loudly, running about, and so forth, after they are eight years old. Stuck in a corner, all movement prohibited. She sits in a corner of the home, head bowed, doing only sewing—doesn't move. She cannot even walk in haste.

One day an eight-year-old girl of a respectable house entered the courtyard and saw a small ladder leaning against the kitchen roof. Tahera (the girl) had no idea what it was there for and unthinkingly climbed up two of the rungs. Her father appeared at just this moment. When he saw her on the ladder he completely lost his mind, grabbed her arm, and yanked her down.

Tahera was an only daughter beloved by her father—beside adoration she had never felt his disapproval; she had never seen his face displeased. Seeing today's raging father-figure with his rough pulling she was so terrified that, trembling violently, she defecated in her clothes!

Because she had to be bathed at an unusual hour, and because she was overcome by extreme terror, Tahera came down with fever that night. A daughter of a great house and a cherished daughter at that, so nothing is spared on medical care. The Civil Surgeon from the far-away central district is called in. In those days (this is forty- to forty-five years back) it was no simple matter to call a doctor. The doctor's fourfold fee, palanquin hire, food, paan, and tobacco for thirty-two palanquin-bearers besides—this is a huge deal.

Despite all this care, Tahera's fever did not subside after three days. Seeing it was hopeless, the doctor left. With a merciless response to her father's harsh treatment, Tahera departed to eternal freedom! (Inna Lillahi Wa Inna Ilayhi Rajioon).[21]

[40]

A wealthy household was ostentatiously decked out for the daughter's wedding. The house resounded with the noise of relatives—nothing was lacking. Many new thatched huts had been put up for the fresh arrivals. One day late in the evening the straw roof of one of these new huts caught fire. Hearing the commotion coming from outside, the servants and retainers assembled to wait in the entry-room of the main house and yelled questions repeatedly: Are you in purdah? Can we come inside? But who would reply from within the women's room? Everyone had been dumbstruck when they saw the fire. Inside the burning hut meantime, the women were discussing whether there was purdah in the courtyard. How could they go outside if young guys were around?

Finally an old woman out of her mind with terror raised her voice: "Hey, idiots! Come and put out the fire! You're asking if we're in purdah at a time like this?"

Everyone then rushed from the porch to extinguish the fire. But the women leaving the burning hut saw a courtyard full of men, went

---

21 Translator's note: this ritual utterance from Quranic Arabic upon someone's death is transliterated into Bengali by Rokeya. The standard translation is "To Allah We belong, and to Him is our return." Quran 2:156.

back inside, and hid behind the wicker door. Luckily, a few courageous young men caught hold of the women and dragged them outside. If not, they'd have been tasty grilled kebabs right there!

[41]

Jaladhar Sen, honored with the title of Ray Bahadur, wrote this in 1928: Purdah in the old days. By old days I do not mean ancient epochs, but the days of our youth—fifty years ago. The image of purdah we saw then, as harsh as it was laughable, is still completely clear to me. I will try to describe a few of these common sights.

One day back then I had gone to Howrah Station for some reason. At the time, I was studying in college. When I got to the platform I saw several footmen clearing a way through the crowd of travelers. I did not dare to approach in case some prince or king was going to board the train; that is why the ruler's soldiers are shoving the unwitting travelers aside! So I stood a little way off awaiting the arrival of this regal personage.

A few minutes passed, the king still had not come. Finally what did I see—a mosquito-net approaches. Four footsoldiers slowly advanced, each one holding up a corner of the mosquito-net. I was speechless at this sight—I had never seen anything like it before. A gentleman was standing beside me. I asked him, "Why are they going about like that with a mosquito-net?" Smiling a little, he said, "Really, you've never seen a mosquito-net on the move before? See how many armed guards there are! They're preserving the honor of the wife of some king or great landlord of Bihar as she gets on to the train. A great man's wife doesn't go around in front of you or me like the rabble. Not even sunlight may touch them!" Saying this, the gentleman began to laugh. Seeing the pomposity of this purdah, I was unable to contain my laughter. Yes, this is purdah's real name—essentially a mosquito-net on the move.

Another time there were preparations going on for ritual bathing in the Ganges. I had gone to the Adya-Shraddha Ghat in Barabazar to watch the splendid crowds and of course—at this ripe age I can freely admit it—to wash away my sins in the Ganges. It was winter, and the time for bathing was at five in the afternoon.

I stood on the ghat watching the splendid crowd and thought, how am I going to bathe in this biting cold. Just then I saw a palanquin, wrapped in cloth from top to bottom, arrive at the ghat. An orderly was gripping each of the palanquin's four corners and an underling attended each of its two doors. It was obvious that this was the wife, daughter, or daughter-in-law of some well-to-do man coming to bathe. No surprise, of course, that women of the great households arrive like this.

But what I saw next was the absolute summit of what is both laughable and pitiable. I had assumed that the palanquin was to be taken down to the river's edge where its passenger would disembark and take her Ganges-bath. How wrong I was! The bearers, the orderlies, and the two underlings—I saw them all take the palanquin and lower it into the water. The water was around chest-height where the palanquin stopped. Next, the bearers plunged the whole palanquin underwater, instantly heaving it up again, and then dragged it back to the riverbank. It departed just as it had arrived. I had to laugh at a palanquin's dip in the Ganges. And it was upsetting to think of the state of whoever was inside it. Those benevolent women shivering in cold wet clothes on this winter's evening. I suppose I was able to see the kind of bathing they get. So that's what we call purdah!

The honorable Mr. Sen laughed at a palanquin's "Ganges-bath." In childhood, we also laughed when we heard of a "palanquin's Brahmaputra River-bath" at Chilamari Ghat. Later in Bhagalpur we also heard about a palanquin's railway trip.

I once saw with my own eyes a thirteen-year-old newlywed girl traveling to her in-laws' place. I remember it quite clearly. Everyone knows how ferociously hot the sun is around Bhagalpur in June.

In June at eight in the morning this newly married young woman in a heavy Banarasi sari, a long veil pulled over her head, boarded a palanquin. Atop the veil was set a heavy headpiece made of flowers covering her brow. After the doors of the palanquin were closed, the palanquin was completely wrapped in gold-stitched red cloth. This palanquin was loaded onto the train's roofless brake van. Like that, young woman roasted and boiled all the way to her in-laws'. All the way to Jashidi!

[42]

The other day (July 7, 1931), a certain woman recounted the two events written below:

Many years ago, one of her great aunts was coming back from a trip to western India. The aunt had sent a telegraph with the time of her arrival at Calcutta. But that day a typhoon tore up all the telegraph lines and there was so much water in Calcutta's streets you could swim! Consequently, no one here got great-aunt's telegram and a palanquin was not sent to collect her from Howrah Station.

In the meantime, great-aunt's reserved traincar arrived at Howrah on time, everyone disembarked, and the luggage was unloaded. But without a palanquin there, great-aunt was completely disinclined to get off the train even though she was wearing a burka. After much arguing and pleading her husband got annoyed and said, "Alright, you stay on the train. We're going." Perceiving the difficulty, great-aunt meekly spoke: "I have a way. Get me down like this." The way was as follows: wrap her entire body in sheets like a bale of cloth and three or four people can haul the bundle off the train. Like that, she was at last loaded onto a horse-carriage.

[43]

A burka-clad married woman got off a train with a bag in her hand. Her husband had her wait in place with all their belongings while he went off to do some business. For some reason, his return was very delayed. Meanwhile, the waiting wife started weeping floods of tears. At the sound of muffled crying and the sight of her trembling body, people gradually began to crowd around. People questioned her kindly, "Do tell us the name of who you're traveling with and we'll go and find him." She points at the sun and then raises her bag to show them. Unable to understand this in the slightest, the people there laughed aloud.

Shortly thereafter, a man ran up. He was out of breath. "What's going on? What's this crowd?" he asked. Once he had heard what happened, he laughingly spoke: "My name is Aftab Beg. So my wife pointed at the sun and then showed you the 'Beg' (bag) in her hand."[22]

---

22 Translator's note: the proper name Aftab means "the sun" in Persian. The report pays an ironic tribute to the woman's linguistic inventiveness as she

[44]

Mr. Sharafaddin Ahmad, B.A. (Aligarh) of Azimabad wrote about the series of incidents below in an Urdu newspaper. (I have been unable to resist the desire to translate them). Hence:

I was in Aligarh until last year. I find the railway station there second-to-none in grandeur on the East India Line, and so I would go there every day on my regular walk. Among the various extraordinary things that appeared before my eyes there was a large number of thirteenth-century burkas. As God is my witness, each and every one of these burkas was in some way absurd. Here I will describe just three among them.

This is the first incident: One day I was pacing the platform of Aligarh Station when I was suddenly shoved from behind. I turned around and saw a lady in a burka standing there who said in an officious tone, "Sir, watch where you're going!" I was extremely amused by this because she had been behind me, so it's easy to figure out whose responsibility it was to watch where they were going. I just made this small remark to her: "Madam, if you would just fix the eye-mesh of your burka so that you can see through it," and smilingly walked off.

[45]

This is the second incident: One day I was at Aligarh station again with a few friends absorbed by the strange and wonderful sights. Just then we heard the sound of an infant weeping close by. We looked all around—nothing to be seen. A little later we again heard an infant screaming right next to us. But after looking this way and that, we could not find a thing. My friends had absolutely no idea. But I had enough experience with the burka to begin investigating. Finally I saw it: a burka-clad lady walking around, the sound of an infant's wailing coming from inside the burka!

What happened was this: the lady had hidden the little child in her burka. It was agitated by the heat and was crying. So no one could see the infant but could only hear its wails. I pointed this spectacle out to my friends. Is it worth recounting the state we were brought to by our laughter?

---

constructs a silent rebus of her husband's name to navigate the moral stricture of not speaking with strangers.

[46]

According to my old habits, I was once again strolling on the platforms of Aligarh Station. I saw a "white circle" (a group in white) approaching me. When it drew near, I saw that right in front was an elderly gentleman holding a betel nut box in one hand and a fan in the other; behind him a few burka-clad women followed, all huddled together. This company had not gone far before it came upon a handcart. Upon colliding with the cart one of the ladies fell, taking the entire party down with her.

Eveningtime, trains coming in, a tumult of travelers—in a place like that, seeing such a shocking tumble on the platform, who wouldn't gawp with curiosity? A large crowd quickly gathered. At first there was a wish to help those who had fallen to the ground; but who can touch a woman? Much pity for the elderly gentleman accompanying them; the poor man alone and all this disaster! Finally I said, "Good sir! Help them up. Why don't you check if these ladies are injured?"

As the poor man began to help them up, I saw that the ladies had all tied their burkas to each other's and had been blindly following the lead of the one in front! The problem before me was: why had the lady in front not seen the danger of the handcart ahead of her? When I took a look at her burka I saw that the mesh on her burka that is supposed to cover the eyes had moved around to the back of her head. It was thus clearly obvious that the lady had been walking forward by guesswork.

The issue now was that when the poor old gentleman tried to help one of the women to stand she would be pulled back down by the others—such that each one he dragged up slipped back out of his hands. After much heaving and pulling like this, the ladies were set upright.

[47]

I would like to speak in the poet's language:
    No poem nor fiction, this is my life,
    No theater-hall, it is nature's house.[23]
    An incident from about three years back, when our first motor-bus

---

23   Translator's note: the quote is probably Rokeya's translation from the Persian poet-philosopher Saadi Shirazi (c. 1209–1292).

was arranged. The day before, one of the female teachers from our school, an Englishwoman, went to the mechanic's shop and returned with the news that the motor-bus was terribly dark... "No way! I'm never getting in that bus." When the bus arrived we saw—its back door was completely covered with fine meshwork and so was the front. If it were not for these three-inch-wide and eighteen-inch-long grilles you could say that the bus was completely airtight.

On the first day, the female students were sent home in the new bus. The assistant returned to report—the bus is really hot—the girls got very agitated on the way home. Some of them threw up. The little ones were weeping in fear of the darkness.

On the second day, when the bus was to bring the students, the aforementioned Englishwoman lowered the slatted blind on the bus door and hung a brightly colored cloth curtain there. Despite this, we saw that when the students arrived at school a few of them were unconscious, several were vomiting, others had headaches, and so on. In the afternoon the Englishwoman lowered the slats on each side of the bus and put up two pieces of fabric curtain. In this way we delivered them home.

That evening Mrs. Mukherjee, an old friend of mine, came to visit. She expressed her pleasure in the various developments at the school— "Your motor-bus is really quite lovely. When I first saw it on the road I thought, is that some wardrobe passing? Shut up on all sides, must be a huge traveling wardrobe. My nephew said, "Oh, aunt! Look at that moving black hole going by![24] Seriously, how can girls sit inside that?"

On the afternoon of the third day, several of the students' mothers came to see me and said, "Your bus really is God's box! You're burying girls alive." Completely helpless, I asked what am I supposed to do. If it wasn't like that you would have said "unveiled transport." They got very annoyed at this and said, "You'll kill to maintain purdah? Our girls aren't coming to school tomorrow." Several girls fainted that day, too. Objections were conveyed through the maidservants of every home: they will no longer come by motor-bus.

The next evening I received four letters in the mail without return addresses. The writer of the English letter signed himself, "Brother-in-Islam." The other three were in Urdu—two anonymous and the fourth

---

24   Translator's note: "moving black hole" is in English typeface in the original.

signed by five people. The subject of each letter was the same—benev-olently wishing the school well, they all wrote that the curtains fixed to the sides of the bus move in the breeze and make the bus unveiled. If the bus is not properly appointed by tomorrow they will, for the further benefit of the school, send nasty, mean, and unpleasant reports to various daily Urdu newspapers. And they will make sure that girls do not go about in such an unveiled bus.

What a predicament—

"Don't catch the snake, the king will kill me—Catch the snake and it will bite."

It is possible that no one has caught a living snake like this by order of the king. For the woman-prisoners I wish to say—

"Why did I come, alas! To this cursed world,
Why begotten in a veiled home!"

TRUE DAWN

Awake mother, sister, daughter—arise, off your beds, come; advance. Listen here, "Muezzin" calls out the azan. Can you not hear the sound of this azan calling, the voice of Allah? Sleep no more; arise, it is night no more, now is true dawn—the muezzin has called the azan. At a time when the whole world's women have awakened, when they have declared war on all kinds of social injustice—when they have become education ministers, doctors, philosophers, scientists, ministers of war, commanders-in-chief, writers, poets, etc., etc.—we Bengali women are laying in deep sleep on the dark, damp floors of domestic dungeons and dying of tuberculosis by the thousands.

We have reserved all the anathemas for ourselves; we do not march in step with the movement of the times. We have sworn an oath resolving not to relinquish our slumber at the azan's call. But this shall no longer be. Sisters! Peek out of the tiny cracks in your own prisons and take a look at the outside world for once!

From the day we came into the world we have heard that we are born slaves, eternal slaves, slaves we will remain.

> O! How sadly sang the poet—
> I can't express the agony within,
> Born as woman for so much sin.

We bear all the world's faults because we are said to be irrational. We have never protested all these wrongs and prejudices because we are said to be mute. We are treated as animals and we feel proud of it.

For a while now our lords and masters have begun to count us as priceless ornaments. Look how many kinds of "Societies for the Protection of Women" are being set up! In reality, since we are living luggage, watchful guardians are needed to prevent us from being stolen! My cursed sisters! Does this not make you feel disgraced? And if it does, then why do you stomach this cruel disgrace in silence?

Let us take a look at ourselves for once—we are likened to animals;

see here, "Society for the Prevention of Cruelty to Animals" next to "Society for the Protection of Women." Could there be a crueler disgrace than this? In any case, this disgrace must end now.

Sisters! Rub your eyes and arise—advance! Beat your chests and say, Mothers! We are not animals; say, Sisters! We are not chattel; say, Daughters! We are not property like a collection of ornaments locked in an iron chest; all proclaim with one voice, We are human! And show in action that we are the best half of all the created world. In reality, we are the mothers of the created world. Build your own associations to defend your demands.

The spread of education is the only medicine to prevent all this injustice. At the very least there must be primary education for young girls! By education I mean genuine, quality education; being able to read a few books or write some lines of verse is not education. The education I ask for is this—one that will enable the exercise of the rights of the citizen, one that will construct ideal daughters, ideal sisters, ideal woman-householders, and ideal mother-figures! I ask for an education doubly focused on mind and body. They must know that they did not come into this world as mere puppets to be adorned with lovely saris, hairclips, and expensive jewelry; rather, they have been born in the shape of women as agents for the accomplishment of a specific responsibility. Their lives are not merely the instruments of a self-sacrificial dedication to the pleasures of idolized husbands. Let them not be on another's leash for basic necessities.

As far as educating the body is concerned, I think that the necessary learning consists of combat with clubs and knives, rice-husking with a dhenki, flour-grinding, and all kinds of work in the home.[1] Rice-husking and wheat-grinding could also solve the widespread food problems of the country. At present, the lack of husked rice and wheatflour is sweeping people away in a flood of death. Compared to aimless leaping about, dancing, and so on, the kinds of bodily exercise I have mentioned are a hundred times better. Morning walks in the open fields are also extremely desirable. It is good that the government is now paying attention to the welfare of children, but we first need to ensure the welfare of their mothers.

---

[1] Translator's note: a dhenki is an indigenous, foot-powered machine for removing rice chaff.

In any case: mothers, sisters, daughters! Sleep no more—arise, advance on the path of what you must do.

ACKNOWLEDGEMENTS

We would first like to express our deep gratitude to our editor and publisher, Mary Bahr of Warbler Press. She has cheered on and contributed to this project every step of the way. We acknowledge the generous support of the Chadha Center for Global India, Princeton University, for funds that made it possible to illustrate the book. We thank Mr. Andalib Elias and Mrs. Suraiya Elias for permission to include Akhtaruzzaman Elias's short biography of Begum Rokeya. Additional thanks are due to Tanya Agathocleous, Zahid Chaudhary, Azra Dawood, Harini Kumar, Deborah Anna Logan, Sarika Persaud, and Arunava Sinha.

www.ingramcontent.com/pod-product-compliance
Lightning Source LLC
Chambersburg PA
CBHW050859180626
46814CB00007B/2797